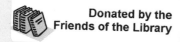

ROBOT WARS

SIGMUND BROUWER

BOOK ONE

DEATH TRAP

TYNDALE HOUSE PUBLISHERS, INC.
CAROL STREAM, ILLINOIS

You can contact Sigmund Brouwer through his Web site at
www.coolreading.com or www.whomadethemoon.com.

Visit Tyndale's exciting Web site for kids at www.tyndale.com/kids.

TYNDALE and Tyndale's quill logo are registered trademarks of Tyndale
House Publishers, Inc.

Death Trap

Previously published as Mars Diaries *Mission 1: Oxygen Level Zero* and
Mars Diaries *Mission 2: Alien Pursuit* under ISBNs 0-8423-4304-0 and
0-8423-4305-9.

Death Trap first published in 2009.

Designed by Mark Anthony Lane II

For manufacturing information regarding this product, please call
1-800-323-9400.

Library of Congress Cataloging-in-Publication Data

Brouwer, Sigmund, date
    Death trap / Sigmund Brouwer.
        p. cm. — (Robot wars)
    Previously pub. in 2000 in two vols. under titles: Mars diaries, Mission 1,
Oxygen level zero; and, Mars diaries, Mission 2, Alien pursuit.
        ISBN 978-1-4143-2309-1 (softcover)
        I. Title.
    PZ7.B79984De 2009
    [Fic]—dc22   2008028714

Printed in the United States of America

15   14   13   12
 9   8   7   6   5

THIS SERIES IS DEDICATED
IN MEMORY OF MARTYN GODFREY.

Martyn, you wrote books that reached all of us kids at heart. You wrote them because you really cared. We all miss you.

FROM THE AUTHOR

We live in amazing times! When I first began writing these Mars journals, not even 40 years after our technology allowed us to put men on the moon, the concept of robot control was strictly something I daydreamed about when readers first met Tyce. Since then, science fiction has been science fact. Successful experiments have now been performed on monkeys who are able to use their brains to control robots halfway around the world!

Suddenly it's not so far-fetched to believe that these adventures could happen for Tyce. Or for you. Or for your children.

With that in mind, I hope you enjoy stepping into a future that could really happen. . . .

SIGMUND BROUWER

JOURNAL ONE

CHAPTER 1

Sandstorm!

Across the plains, the black shell of the gigantic dome gleamed in late-afternoon sunshine. It was beautiful against the red soil, laden with iron oxides, and the faded rose-colored Martian sky. From the bottom of the mountain where I stood, it took less than an hour's trek across the plains to reach it—in good weather.

But we would not get that hour. Sand rattled hard against my titanium casing, warning me of how little time remained. Much less than we needed.

I turned my head to the left, into the wind that raked the sand across me. A huge dark wall lifted from the north of the plains, a blanket of doom that covered more and more of the sky. Winds of near-hurricane force lifted tons of red sand particles. Already the front edge of the storm reached out to us. In less than half an hour, those tons of sand would begin to cover me and the three scientists I had been sent out of the dome to find.

"Home base," I called into my radio. "This is Rescue Force One. Please make contact. Home base. This is Rescue Force One. Please make contact."

There was no answer. Just like there had been no answer the other hundred times I'd tried in the last half hour.

A solar flare must have knocked out the satellite beam. The sun was about 140 million miles away, so weak and so far from Mars that on winter nights, the temperature here dropped to minus 200 degrees Fahrenheit. Yet all it took was a storm on the surface of the sun to fire out electromagnetic streams nearing the speed of light, and communication systems through the entire solar system would pay the price.

"Home base," I said. "This is Rescue Force One. Please make contact."

One of the scientists walked in front of me, blocking my view of the base. He leaned down and pushed his helmet visor into my forward video lens. "What are we going to do?" he shouted.

He did not have to shout. I could hear him clearly. Nor did he have to walk around in front of me. I could have seen him just as easily with my rear video lens. Or one of my side lenses.

"Forward," I said. "We cannot stop."

"No! We must make shelter."

Did he think I had not thought of this already? Standard procedure in dealing with a sandstorm was to go to high ground, unfold an emergency pop-up blanket, and crawl beneath it. The pop-up blanket made a miniature dome that would easily provide shelter for as many days as it took the storm to pass. But fools who used the pop-up blanket on low ground would be buried by the sand, never to be found again.

"Forward," I said. "Follow me."

"That's easy for you!" he hollered. "You're just a stupid machine!"

He was correct both times. It would be easy for me to travel in a sandstorm, and I was just a machine. But he was also wrong. I was more than a machine. And I was not stupid. I knew plenty.

I knew that during each Martian fall and winter, the carbon dioxide gas in the atmosphere froze out of the air and onto the ground, making a giant hood of frost that covered from the pole to the equator. I knew that as spring arrived, the difference in temperatures between the sun-warmed soil and the retreating ice made for fierce winds. I knew these strong winds were so monstrous that sometimes sandstorms covered the entire planet. I knew if we took shelter, we might be trapped for days.

I also knew that the last scientist had only 10 hours of

oxygen left in his tank. If we took shelter, he would die long before the storm ended.

"One of you will die if we stop," I said. "If we continue, all of you will survive."

"We'll get lost in the storm! No one survives a sandstorm."

"No," I insisted. "My navigation system is intact. We will link ourselves by cable, and I will maintain direction. All you need to do is follow."

"No!" he yelled. "Not through a sandstorm!"

"Listen," I said, "if we stop, he has no chance."

"Should three of us die instead of one?" The scientist picked up a rock and tried to smash it against my head. But since he wore a big atmosphere suit and was very slow, I moved out of the way easily.

He picked up another rock and threw it at me. I put up my arms to protect my video lenses, and the rock clanged off my elbows.

The other two scientists watched, doing nothing. They were very tired. I had rescued them from the bottom of a giant sinkhole where they had been stranded for two days.

The first scientist picked up another rock to throw. It was a big rock. Even though his suit made him clumsy, he would be able to throw it hard. Mars has very little gravity compared to Earth. A person throwing a rock the size of a grapefruit on Earth could easily throw a rock the size of a basketball on Mars.

What was I going to do? If I let the scientist with the rocks force us to stop and put up a shelter, one of them would die. But if I grabbed the scientist with the rock in my sharp metal claws, I would most certainly poke a hole in his space suit. With an atmosphere of 95 percent carbon dioxide, he would die within minutes.

Either way, it didn't look like I could find a way to make sure all three scientists made it back to the dome alive. I would fail in my task. I could not allow that.

Another rock clanged off my leg.

"No!" I said. "No!" This was getting worse. If I ran off to protect myself, then all three of them might die. But if I stayed to try to protect them, one of those rocks might smash and disable me. Which would mean all of them might die. I couldn't decide what to do.

The scientist threw another rock. It hit my shoulder.

A huge blast of sand swept over us. For a moment, I could see nothing in any direction from my four video lenses.

In the instant the air cleared again, I saw the scientist with another rock in his fist. But it was too late. Out of the swirling sand he appeared, aiming the rock toward my video lenses.

The rock smashed down.

The rose-colored sky tilted. The red soil zoomed toward me. Then everything went black. . . .

CHAPTER 2

"Ouch," I said.

I opened my eyes to the square, sterile room of the computer simulation lab. I was under the dome, not outside of it, stuck in a raging sandstorm. That was the good news.

The bad news was that although no rock had actually hit my body, my head hurt. That's the way it is with a virtual-reality program. It's like a computer game. Except you're actually in the game. Instead of watching your players get knocked out, it happens in a small way to you.

I pulled the surround-sight helmet off my head. My hair was slick with sweat. The concentration it took to move the virtual-reality robot controls by flexing my own muscles was hard work. It didn't help that I was also wearing a one-piece jacket and gloves, wired with thousands of tiny cables that reacted to every movement I made. I'd been in the computer program for five hours, and that jacket held every scrap of my body heat.

"Ouch is right," Rawling said, looking up from his own screen where he sat at a desk across the cramped room from me. "My readout shows he cracked three video lenses and shocked your computer drive. Basically he killed you. A human defeating a robot."

Rawling McTigre, one of the two medical doctors under the dome, was stocky and in his mid 40s. He had been a quarterback at his university back on Earth when he was younger, and his wide shoulders showed it. His short, dark hair was streaked with gray. He said his hair had turned gray from trying to look after me. I spent so much time with him that there were days when I wished he were my father. I mean, because voice-to-voice calls were far too costly as my real father traveled between Earth and Mars, and because the round trip took so long, all I really had for a father was a photo of some guy in a pilot's space suit.

"What were you thinking out there?" Rawling asked.

"Thinking? I didn't have time to think," I responded. "I'd spent four hours tracking them down, and suddenly the one goofball decides he doesn't want to be rescued. Besides, who programmed the sandstorm into this rescue operation? Wasn't it bad enough one guy is running low on oxygen and the satellite communications are down? What was next—a short circuit that left my robot unit with only one arm or one video lens in operation?"

"Tyce, Tyce, Tyce." Rawling shook a good-natured finger at me. "I don't remember anyone ever making it to stage five of that program. You have this gift, this talent, this—"

"You're about to lecture me, aren't you?" I said, sighing. "You always start your lectures by giving me a compliment. Then you let me have it."

He laughed. "You've got me figured out. But I have to discuss your mistakes and what you can learn from them. If I don't, how will you be able to control the perfect virtual-reality robot?"

"That's another thing," I said. I was hot and thirsty. I was mad at the scientist who'd knocked me out with a rock. I was grumpy. "Why do I need to control the perfect virtual-reality robot?"

Rawling gave me a strange look.

"I've been thinking about that a lot lately," I said, pressing forward. "I'm not the one who wants me to be perfect. You are."

He still said nothing. I wondered if he was mad at me.

"Don't get me wrong," I responded quickly. "It's fun to become part of the program and pretend I'm actually outside the dome. But I want the real thing. I want to get outside. I want to look up and actually see the sky and the sunset. Not just have it projected into my surround-sight helmet. I want—"

"Tyce," Rawling said quietly, "look down."

Even though I knew what was there, I looked down. At my wheelchair. At useless, crippled legs. At pants that never got ripped or dirty because I was always sitting, legs motionless, in my wheelchair.

"I know. I know," I said sadly. "Sinking into Martian sand would eat up these wheels in less than a minute. But I can't let that stop me."

He stared at me.

"You're the one," I murmured, "who always tells me this is only a handicap if I let it be a handicap."

Dome horns began to blare in short bursts. I counted four blares.

Four blares? That meant . . .

"A call for everyone to assemble," Rawling said, reading my mind.

The dome director was going to speak to all 200 of us under the dome at the same time. That hadn't happened since it looked like an asteroid might hit Mars, and that had been five years ago.

"I was afraid of this," Rawling muttered. He took my surround-sight helmet off my lap and set it beside the computer on the desk in front of me. "This may be your last computer run for a while."

"What?"

"It means a techie has confirmed my oxygen readings. Director Steven is going to tell all of us to avoid using electricity on anything except totally necessary activities. At least until we get our problem fixed."

"Oxygen readings? Problem fixed?" This sounded serious. Too serious. Just as serious as the look on Rawling's face.

"Over the last week," he explained, "and during routine checkups, scientists and techies complained to me about being too tired. And I've been tired myself."

Now that he mentioned it, my arms didn't feel that strong after pushing my wheelchair across the dome. Most of the time my arms were very strong, because I had to use them like my legs if I wanted my wheelchair to go anywhere.

"But I couldn't find anything wrong with them," Rawling continued. "So without telling anyone, I took some oxygen readings. The dome was down 10 percent in oxygen levels."

"Ten percent!"

"That was three days ago," he said. "I didn't want to spread panic, so I kept it to myself and asked the director to get a techie to confirm it. I hoped I was doing the readings wrong."

The dome horns began to blast again. Four blares.

Rawling waited until they finished. "I guess I wasn't wrong. Worse, today my own readings showed we are now down 12 percent. Somehow the oxygen generators are failing little by little, and it looks like the problem is getting worse."

CHAPTER 3

With time running out, Mom wants me, Tyce Sanders, to write all that is happening in a journal for people to read on Earth when we are gone. We'll store it on a hard drive here and have it sent by satellite e-mail to the Internet systems of Earth schools. That way kids who have been following the Mars Project will get a chance to know about our last days. She thinks it will mean more to people coming from a kid my age than from any scientist.

But I hardly know where to begin. I mean, earlier this afternoon, my biggest worry was whether I could conquer a virtual-reality program where I controlled a super-robot. Now, the oxygen level in the colony is dropping so fast that all of us barely have five days to live.

I stopped and stared at my computer screen. Writing is not easy for me. I used to think that because I had a hard time with it, it meant I was dumb. Rawling laughed one day when I told him that. He said I was not dumb. He said most people found writing difficult, and it just took practice. He said sometimes adults forget that, and they expect their kids to be good writers instantly.

Hearing him say that made me feel better. And it made sense. It was unfair when adults looked at a kid's writing and expected that kid to be as good at it as adults who have been writing for years and years. So now I'm not as afraid to put my thoughts onto a computer screen.

I began to type again on the keyboard in my lap.

First, today's date: AD 06.20.2039, Earth calendar. It's been a little more than 14 years since the dome was established in 2025. When I think about it, that means some of the scientists and techies in the dome were my age around the year 2000, even though the last millennium seems like ancient history. Of course, kids back then didn't have to deal with water shortage wars and one-world governments and an exploding population that meant we had to find a way to colonize Mars.

Things have become so desperate on Earth that already 500 billion dollars have been spent on this project, which seems like a lot until you do the math and realize that's only about 10 dollars for every person on the planet.

Kristy Sanders, my mom, used to be Kristy Wallace until she married my father, Chase Sanders. They teamed up with nearly 200 men and women specialists from all countries across the world when the first ships left Earth. I was just a baby, so I can't say I remember, but from what I've been told, those first few years of assembling the dome were heroic. Now we live in comfort. I've got a computer that lets me download e-entertainment from Earth by satellite, and the gardens that were planted when I was a kid make parts of the dome seem like a tropical garden. It isn't a bad place to live.

But now it could become a bad place to die.

Today Blaine Steven, the dome director, called everyone together and told us that the gigantic solar panels that cover most of the ceiling of the dome are failing to make enough electricity to run the dome and provide all our oxygen. He said if we cut back our use of electricity to only what is

absolutely needed, we can use the rest of the electricity to make more oxygen. He warned that this
alone would not be enough. But the reserve oxygen
in the dome's spare tanks will get us through the
last few days until the supply ship arrives.

So no extra electricity can be used on anything. The only reason I'm able to use my computer
is because it's running on battery. It means we
won't even use electricity for running showers. It's
better to be smelly and able to smell the smelliness,
Director Steven said, than to be clean and dead.
Everyone agreed.

Director Steven also said that most work
under the dome would be shut down. He said people
should rest and sleep and read e-books as much as
possible because resting bodies use less oxygen.
He said if all of us joined together we had a really
good chance of surviving.

Let me say this to anyone on Earth who might
read this. If, like me, you have legs that don't work,
Mars, with its lower gravity pull, is probably a better place to be than Earth.

That's only a guess, of course, because I haven't
had the chance to compare Mars' gravity to Earth's
gravity. In fact, I'm the only person in the entire
history of mankind who has never been on Earth.

I'm not kidding.

You see, I'm the first person born on Mars. Everyone else here came from Earth nearly eight Martian years ago—15 Earth years to you—as part of the first expedition to set up a colony. The trip took eight months, and during this voyage my mother and father fell in love. Mom is a leading plant biologist. Dad is a space pilot. They were the first couple to be married on Mars. And the last, for now. They loved each other so much that they married by exchanging their vows over radio phone with a preacher on Earth. When I was born half a Mars year later—which now makes me 14 Earth years old—it made things so complicated on the colony that it was decided there would be no more marriages and babies until the colony was better established.

I stopped again. Because Mom tells me that much of the Mars Project has been explained so often in the media and in schools, I knew I didn't have to go into detail about the colony itself. I guessed everybody on Earth already knew that Phase 1 was to establish the dome. Phase 2, which we were just about to start, was to grow plants outside the dome so more oxygen could be added to the atmosphere. The long-range plan—which would take over a hundred years—was to make the entire planet a place for humans to live outside the dome.

People on Earth desperately needed the room. Already the planet had too many people on it. If Mars could be made a new colony, then Earth could start shipping people here to live. If not, new wars might begin, and millions of people would die from war or starvation or disease.

I wondered, though, if people really understood how different it was to live under a dome nearly 50 million miles away from the planet Earth.

I turned back to my keyboard.

What was complicated about a baby on Mars?

Let me put it this way. Because of planetary orbits, spaceships can reach Mars only every three years. (Only four ships have arrived since I was born.) And for what it costs to send a ship from Earth, cargo space is expensive. Very, very expensive. Diapers, baby bottles, cribs, and carriages are not exactly a priority for interplanetary travel.

I did without all that stuff. In fact, my wheelchair isn't even motorized, because every extra pound of cargo costs something like 10,000 dollars.

Just like I did without a modern hospital when I was born. So when my spinal column twisted funny during birth and damaged the nerves to my legs, there was no one to fix them. Which is why I'm in a wheelchair.

But it could be worse. On Earth, I'd weigh 110 pounds. Here, I'm only 42 pounds, so I don't have to fight gravity nearly as hard as Earth kids.

I thought about my father. I felt like I hardly knew him or he knew me because he didn't stay long between trips to Earth and back. For a long time I was always angry when I thought about this, because, from what I've read, most kids get to grow up with their fathers. And most kids get to grow up using their legs. But I've decided not to waste time caring about him or about what has happened to my legs.

I tapped at my keyboard, slowly putting more words together.

When my body and arms aren't weak from lack of oxygen, the lower gravity does make it easy to get around in my wheelchair.

The other good thing is that I never have to travel far. Not like on Earth, where you can go in one direction for thousands of miles. Here, all 200 of us—mainly scientists and techies, the name we give technicians—live under a sealed dome that might cover four football fields. (I know all this about Earth because of the DVD-gigarom books I scan for hours every day.)

When I'm not being taught by my computer or

Rawling McTigre, I spend my time wheeling around the paths beneath the colony dome. I know every scientist and techie by first name. I know every path past every minidome, the small, dark plastic huts where people live in privacy from the others. Between the solar panels that crowd the ceiling I've seen every color of Martian sky through the superclear plastic of the main dome above us. I've spent hours listening to sandstorms rattle over us. I've . . .

. . . I've got to go. Mom's calling me to join her for mealtime.

I hit the Save button on my keyboard. There would be plenty of time later to report more on our oxygen crisis, millions of miles away from rescue.

CHAPTER 4

Our minidome, like everyone else's, had two office-bedrooms with a common living space in the middle. Mom wasn't able to use her second room as an office because that had become my bedroom. We didn't need a kitchen, because we never had anything to cook. Instead, a microwave hung on the far wall; it was used to heat nutrient tubes. Another door at the back of the living space led to a small bathroom. It wasn't much. From what I've read about Earth homes, our minidome had less space than two average bedrooms. And I could only dream about having a backyard and fence and garden the way I'd seen in e-photos.

Mom was waiting for me in one of the chairs in the common area. She had thick dark hair that was cut short, like an upside-down bowl. She didn't care much what she looked like—especially during the long, long months while my father was gone between refueling stops on Mars. It meant more to have a hairstyle that didn't take much fussing and gave her as much time as possible for her science. As the leading plant biologist on the station, Mom had a big job: to genetically alter Earth plants so they could grow on Mars.

She gave me a tired smile—the 14-hours-of-hard-scientific-work smile. I gave her one in return.

"How are you doing with your journal?" she asked, like this was just another normal day.

"Fine," I said, like this was just another normal day. "What's for supper?"

Dying was funny. Not funny ha-ha. Funny strange. Everyone thought about it all the time, but nobody wanted to talk about it.

I grunted as I pushed my wheelchair toward her. It was getting harder and harder to move it. I worried that pretty soon I might not be able to move it at all.

Mom stood at the microwave and hit the buttons.

As I waited for the seconds to count down, I did what I always did whenever I had to wait. I reached down to the pouch hanging from the armrest of my wheelchair and pulled out my three red juggling balls. I began to juggle, keeping all three in the air so it looked like one blur. Some people twiddle their thumbs. Me, I like to juggle. Rawling says I learned it because it's something athletic I can do better than most people who aren't crippled. He's probably right.

The microwave dinged that it was ready.

I caught the juggling balls and put them in the pouch. With effort, I pushed my wheelchair toward Mom.

She handed me a plastic nutrient tube about the size of a chocolate bar. Red.

"Spaghetti and meatballs?" I asked.

She nodded. I've never tasted real spaghetti and meatballs, so I have to take Mom's word for it that the nute-tube stuff is not nearly as good as the real thing.

As usual, she prayed over it.

As usual, I didn't.

As usual, it made her sad.

"Our oxygen level is dropping faster and faster," Mom said softly. "How can I convince you to place your faith in God? If we have only a month left . . ."

"I only believe what I can see or measure," I said. In the colony, I was surrounded by scientists. All their experiments were on data that could be seen—and measured.

"But faith is the confident hope in things unseen," she insisted, a bit teary-eyed. "Otherwise it wouldn't be a matter of faith. We don't see your dad, but we know he loves us, no matter where his cargo ship is. Faith in God is like that."

Right, I thought. I wasn't going to tell her that it wasn't

easy to love a space-pilot father you never saw. And it wasn't easy to believe he loved me, either.

"Mom—" we had argued this so much that I decided to stick with the same old argument—"you can't make me believe in God. If you want me to pretend, I will."

"No," she said, with her mouth tight the way it is when she's vexed. "I always want you to be honest with me."

"There you go," I said. "End of argument."

I ripped off the top of my nute tube. Most of the scientists needed to use a knife or scissors. I didn't since I had developed a lot of strength in my arms and hands.

I guzzled the red paste, then tossed it on the table. "I'm going." Mom and I were good friends, but we were both grumpy from our argument about God and from the oxygen problem. I needed time by myself.

She didn't ask me where I was going. She didn't need to. There isn't much room in the dome for me to get lost. And everyone knows I'm a telescope freak. I spent any spare time I had on the third-level deck at the telescope.

By the time I wheeled to the center of the dome 15 minutes later, I was sweating from the effort. Before, it would have taken only a couple of minutes and hardly any muscle power. This oxygen thing was scary. But what could I do about it?

The deck was dim because all but the most-needed lights had been shut down. Just another reminder of the oxygen problem.

Around me, men and women scientists walked slowly on the paths, going from minidome to minidome for whatever business they had. They nodded or said hello as they passed me.

In my wheelchair, I nodded and said hello back. Other than that, as I rolled along, I just stared upward at the stars above the dome. Other people on other expeditions might one day explore the planet outside. Not us. For starters, I wondered if we'd be dead soon. Dad was piloting the next cargo ship, and it wouldn't arrive for five days. One day after the colony dome ran out of oxygen.

I kept staring upward. My gaze drifted to the giant dark solar panels that hung just below the clear roof of the dome. These solar panels, which turned the energy of sunlight into electricity, were killing us. Part of this electricity powered our computers and other equipment. Most of the electricity, though, flowed as a current into the water of the oxygen tank. The electrical current broke the water—H_2O—into the gases of hydrogen and oxygen, two parts hydrogen for every one part of oxygen. The hydrogen was used as fuel for some of the generators. The oxygen, of course, we breathed.

But something was wrong with the panels. Nobody could figure it out. Taken down and tested, they worked perfectly. But back up at the roof, the panels were making less and less electricity each day. With less power, we had less oxygen. It was that simple. I focused upward, thinking about that.

Then it hit me. It wasn't the panels. It was the sunlight. What if the panels worked fine, but they weren't getting enough sunlight?

And I thought I knew why!

I spun my wheelchair around and began to move as fast as I could toward the director's minidome.

At that moment all of the dome's lights snapped off. The hum of the generator quit.

In total silence and darkness, I froze.

Then I heard a scream.

Unless I was wrong, that scream had come from the direction of my minidome.

CHAPTER 5

Within seconds, the total blackness inside the dome was filled with flashlight beams, making the air look like a giant confused sword fight of lights.

I still didn't move. I didn't have a flashlight. I couldn't see where to go. In a wheelchair, the last thing you want to do is hit something that will knock you flying. When you can't use your legs, it's embarrassing to have to crawl along the ground and try to pull yourself up into the wheelchair again.

More screaming reached my ears. A strange blue glow began to appear in the dome, like neon ice melting in all directions.

The emergency backup lights were on. In the glow, I saw a figure running toward me, with other figures chasing it.

"Hey!" I shouted.

Shouting was a very dumb thing to do. It alerted the running person to the fact that I was in my wheelchair and waiting.

Whoever it was turned and shielded his face with his arm as he kept running toward me. In the weird glow of the backup lights, I didn't have a chance of figuring out who it was. He darted sideways to go around my wheelchair.

Sticking out my arm, I tried to stop him. Since people were chasing him, they probably had a reason for wanting to stop him.

That was another dumb thing to do. If I'd actually grabbed him, the force of his momentum could have ripped my arm off at my shoulder.

He passed me. Other dark figures got closer as they kept chasing him.

"Hey!" I shouted, louder. This time I did want to be seen. Getting trampled in my wheelchair is not my favorite evening activity.

"Hey!" I shouted one more time—and not because I wanted to warn anyone. This time it was because my wheelchair was suddenly moving.

The person behind me had given me a shove! He wanted me and my wheelchair to block the people chasing him.

I tried squeezing my brakes, but it was too late. I was on one of the sidewalk paths between minidomes. There was hardly any room to move around me on either side.

There must have been 10 people chasing this guy. And with 10 people all running like crazy, with hardly any room on the path to begin with, it's not fun to be the wheelchair that flies directly into the crowd.

Bang!

Something hard hit me in the face.

I tumbled out of my wheelchair and skidded on my chin into the side of a minidome. Two other people stepped on me and tripped. Someone behind them fell right on top of me. Then something else hit me on top of my head—someone's knee, I found out later. It mashed my face into the floor of the dome. I cracked my forehead in a thump that sounded like wood against concrete.

After that, I didn't remember anything else, except that slowly it got darker and darker and the noises became quieter and quieter until I finally faded out completely.

CHAPTER 6

It smelled like someone was ramming a bottle of bleach up my nose.

Smelling salts.

It snapped me right out of my black daze.

I woke up with Rawling on one side of me and my mother looking down, worried, from the other side. I was on my back on an examining table in the medical emergency room.

"Hey," I said with a croak. "Someone turned the lights back on."

Mom sighed with relief, smiled, and wiped my face with a cold, wet cloth.

"Welcome back, scout," Rawling said. "Now you know what it would be like to play football."

"And be the football?" I groaned. "See, I told you it's a dumb game."

Rawling and I argue about that all the time. He's got a DVD-gigarom collection of Super Bowl games, and he loves watching them. I can't figure it out. A bunch of guys running into each other and a bunch more people screaming at them.

"What happened out there?" I asked. "I was just minding my own business when it went dark. I heard screams and saw this guy getting chased and then—"

"He pushed you into the people chasing him and got away."

"Nobody gets away from anybody in this dome," I said. "It's too small."

"Whoever it was," Rawling replied, "got away long enough to stop running and find a way to mingle with the crowds. That's the best way to hide in here. Just look like everybody else. He's not a stranger, since the only humans on Mars are the ones already living under the dome."

Mom asked, "Did you get a look at his face?"

"Couldn't see anything," I said. "What did he do?"

"Nothing," Rawling said. "At least nothing we can figure out."

"I heard shouting in the dark."

"That came from the minidome next to ours," Mom said. "Someone pushed in one of the walls when the lights went out."

Not that collapsing a wall would be difficult. Although

the minidomes were built to act as temporary air-sealed shelters if the big dome ever temporarily lost its atmosphere, the walls were made of lightweight, rigid plastic.

"I don't get it," I said.

"Neither do we. The director has a security detail looking into it. Turn over."

"Huh?"

"You mean 'pardon me,' right?" Mom said, grinning at me.

"Yes, Mom," I said. "Pardon me?"

"Turn over," Rawling repeated. "I need to examine your back."

"It's my head that hurts," I said.

"Turn over," he insisted. "Doctor knows best."

Slowly I managed to flip myself over on the examining table. It would have been faster for Rawling to help me, but he knew that was one thing I liked to do for myself.

Rawling lifted my shirt and ran his fingers up my back. He stopped near my neck and felt around. "Does this hurt?"

"No."

He took his hands out from under my shirt and squeezed my neck, just above my shoulders. "Does this hurt?"

"No. I told you already. It's my head that hurts."

Rawling moved my head gently from side to side. "Can you feel any pain in your neck when I do this?"

"Just my head."

"Good."

"Good? You like it that my head hurts?"

"Good that it doesn't appear you've done any damage to your back and shoulders. Come back tomorrow, and I'll take some X-rays to be sure."

"Doc," I said, rolling over and sitting up, "why do you do this same exam of my back and shoulders every time I come in for a checkup?"

Seeming startled, Rawling glanced over at Mom. She looked at me and then back at the doctor. She shook her head, as if she was telling him no.

"I worry about your spinal column," Rawling said. "It's not as strong as it should be." He dropped his gaze.

Rawling never did that unless he was uncomfortable. I wondered if, for the first time, he was lying to me.

But I couldn't imagine why. And I couldn't imagine that Mom was in on the lie. Things were getting weirder all the time.

CHAPTER 7

It's me again. Tyce. Remember, I was writing to all of you on Earth and got called away to supper. It's now the middle of the next day. Things got crazy here, and I didn't make it back to my computer right away like I planned.

Last night I was going to tell you more about living under the dome. Now it looks like all I have to write about is dying under the dome.

Someone stole a bunch of reserve oxygen tanks. My friend and doctor, Rawling, said it took three people to do it. One person shut down the generator so the entire dome was dark. Another person pushed down a minidome and ran around in the dark with people chasing him. During this distraction, a third person used a trolley to take the reserve tanks.

I paused to rest my fingers. I thought about what I was writing. The strangest part was that security had searched the entire dome a dozen times and couldn't find those tanks. They are the size of scuba-diving tanks I've read about in my DVD-gigarom books. Except these tanks have super-compressed air and last 10 people about 2 days each.

Twenty tanks were stolen. There should be no possible way for 20 tanks to be hidden. Not when the minidomes are so small a person couldn't even hide one tank.

I wondered too about the three people who stole the tanks. As soon as they start to use the noisy tanks, they'll be found. Unless they're going to wait until the rest of us are no longer breathing.

I wondered how they'd explain this when the spaceship finally arrived. My father and the other pilots would walk in, and the people who stole the tanks would be the only ones healthy and living.

The latest news flash: Director Steven now says that because of the stolen tanks, even if we don't use any electricity in the next three days and even if all of us sleep all the time, we'll still run short of oxygen one day before the ship arrives.

I began to type again.

This morning Rawling told me that some other people had a secret meeting. He was invited because he's a doctor. He was also invited because if Rawling agrees to something, most other people in the dome will agree. They trust him.

Well, the meeting is no longer a secret.

Rawling got very angry with what they suggested. He not only refused to join them, but he brought their idea immediately to the attention of Director Steven and wants them arrested.

You see, the people in this meeting did some math. They say that even after the oxygen tanks were stolen, there is enough oxygen under the dome for 180 people to survive until the ship arrives. This means the dome needs 20 fewer people in it than it has now.

The people in this meeting want to draw names to see which 20 people should die.

CHAPTER 8

"Tyce, as you can imagine, I have very little time for anything else but the oxygen problem," Director Steven said. "As it is, I can only fit five minutes into my schedule for you. I hope this meeting is as important as you insisted."

Short and wide, Director Steven has thick, wavy, gray hair. He likes to run his hands through it as he talks. I think he does that because he likes to remind himself that he has way more hair than most people his age. He's over 60, and a lot of the 40- and 50-year-old scientists are going bald.

"Yes, sir," I said. I stayed very polite, even though I'd been asking to see him all day. The more I thought about my theory, the more I knew I was right. All the oxygen problems could be solved. "I think I might know what's wrong with the solar panels."

Behind his desk, Director Steven leaned back in his chair. His office is the size of most entire minidomes. He also has framed paintings of Earth scenes, like sunsets and mountains, on his wall. No one else has paintings. Cargo's too expensive. "So tell me, young Tyce, what do you know that all our experts here don't know?"

By his tone of voice, I knew right then that I should have had Rawling bring my idea to Director Steven.

Rawling once told me that some people didn't like me simply because my unexpected birth here had taken time and resources that weren't planned. He had explained that Director Steven was one of those people, especially because he acted like the entire Mars Project was his. The trouble was, this far from Earth, with him as commander, it basically was his project. So everybody had to do what he said.

"Sir," I began. Now that I was here, it was too late to turn around. "I don't think the problem is with the solar panels."

"I see," he said sarcastically, running his fingers through his hair. "So it's just our imagination that the dome is running out of oxygen."

It wasn't fair that he treated me like I was just a stupid kid, not when I'd been forced to think and act like all the adults around me for as long as I could remember. If any of the adults in the dome had come in, Director Steven at least would have listened to them with respect. But I knew

I couldn't say this, of course, or he'd get mad and tell me to leave. My point was too important.

"What I mean," I said as firmly as I could, "is that the techies have taken the solar panels down twice from the railings and found absolutely nothing wrong with them."

"Thank you for telling me something I already know," Director Steven said mockingly. "You now have three minutes of my time left."

I tried to keep a polite smile on my face. "If it's not the panels that are broken in some way, then maybe the problem is the sunlight."

"This is good," he said, leaning forward. "Very good."

"It is?"

"You have been kind enough to help me understand this completely." Director Steven shook his head in disgust. "Now I've discovered we have to fix the sun."

"Sir, that's not what I mean. What if there is something blocking the panels from getting the sun?"

"Clouds? On Mars? Hardly. There's no atmosphere. Although that's our goal, we still haven't even found plants that will survive out there long enough to begin to create an atmosphere."

"What about the dome itself?" I asked. "In my virtual-reality computer sessions, the protective visors get scratched because of sandstorms. Maybe over the years Martian sand has done that to the dome, and less sunlight is getting through."

Director Steven stood abruptly and strode out from behind his desk. In his white lab coat, he appeared even larger than he was. From my wheelchair, I had to lean my head back to look up at him. I hated doing that because it made me feel small—and weak.

"Do you think we are stupid?" he thundered, looming over me. "Do you think when we designed this project we didn't think of that? The glass of the dome is as hard as diamonds. It was made to withstand the impact of small asteroids. A million years from now, the glass will still be as clear as the day it was made."

"I . . . I . . . was only trying to help," I said.

"You think you know all the answers," he said, his face red and furious. "Instead, you know nothing." He leaned down in front of me and stared closely into my face. "Dr. McTigre keeps me informed of your progress in the virtual-reality program, you know. He told me how you failed yesterday. How the scientist attacked you instead of letting you lead all of them across the plains in a sandstorm. And let me tell you why. It's because you didn't bother to explain how you could do it. You just assumed if you told them something, that's the way it was and they should listen. You should have learned yesterday that that technique doesn't work—before you wasted my time today. You're supposed to be smarter than that. Or are you?"

I kept my head as steady as I could. I knew nothing I

could say would make a difference. I should have known bet-ter than to try to talk to Director Steven on my own. I should have remembered that he'd made it clear on numerous occa-sions that he couldn't be bothered by me—and that my pres-ence alone under the dome had already bothered him enough over the years.

Director Steven's cold blue eyes bored into mine. "Now please leave," he said flatly. "I have better things to do than let some teenager tell me how to run my project."

I went. Slowly. My wheelchair seemed like it was glued in place. Were my arms that dead already from lack of oxygen?

I'm not sure if I cared. My ears burned from anger and embarrassment.

Why did Director Steven seem to bristle every time he saw me? Did he dislike me that much? And if so, why? Was there something wrong with me?

CHAPTER 9

That night, after a very quiet and short supper, I decided to go up to the third deck, where the telescope was, because I wanted to be alone.

The main level of the dome held the minidomes and labs. One level up, a walkway about 10 feet wide circled the inside of the dome walls. People mostly used the walkway for exercise, jogging in circles above the main floor below. Not me, of course. The techies had built a ramp for my wheelchair, and the only reason I ever went to the second level was to reach the third and smallest level of the dome, which anyone, including me in a wheelchair, could reach by a narrow catwalk from the second level.

This third level was centered at the top the dome. The floor of it was a circle only 15 feet wide. It hung directly below the ceiling, above the exact middle of the main level. Here, on the deck of the third level, a powerful telescope was perched beneath a round bubble of clear, thick glass that stuck up from the black glass that made up the rest of the dome. From there, the massive telescope gave an incredible view of the solar system.

It was getting more difficult to push my wheelchair, and I needed to stop for breath a couple times. Each gasp I took reminded me of how little time was left before the oxygen ran out.

I wondered if I was breaking the new rule about resting to save oxygen. No one was jogging on the walkway. Below me, as I slowly wheeled up the catwalk, it was quiet on the main level of the dome. Most people were inside their mini-domes. But I decided that if I didn't have long to live, I didn't want to waste time I could spend with the telescope.

Tonight I not only wanted to take my mind off the oxygen problem in this death trap, but I wanted to forget what Director Steven had said to me. Maybe I did think I was too smart. Maybe I did bug people. Wondering about all that and thinking about how useless and young he thought I was, I didn't like myself much, either.

The best way to escape the dome and myself was with the telescope on the third level. Because if my crippled body wasn't able to take me places, at least my eyes and mind and imagination could. For me, the telescope was freedom, something that let me travel a billion miles across the universe with a single sweep across the sky.

I rolled into place at the eyepiece of the telescope where the dome astronomer usually sat. I allowed myself a sad smile as I lifted my hands to the controls. The one good thing about useless legs was that you never needed to look for a chair.

I let out a deep breath as I reached the telescope controls. The power to the computer controls of the telescope was down as part of the director's energy-saving program, but I knew how to find different stars and planets without the computer map. After all, the solar system was my backyard.

I brought the telescope into focus. The black of the universe and the brightness of the millions and millions of stars hit me with incredible clearness. It was a clearness no one would ever see on Earth, where the air and the clouds and the particles of pollution take away the sharpness of telescopes. But not on Mars, which has nearly no atmosphere. When you sit at the telescope, it feels like you can reach out and grab the stars.

In the next 30 seconds, Terror and Panic passed by me.

To anyone under the dome, that was an old joke. The names of the two moons of Mars are Deimos and Phobos. These Greek names translate to *terror* and *panic*, because Mars was named after an ancient god of war.

But don't think of these moons like the one that circles

Earth. Deimos and Phobos are tiny moons, chunks of rock not even 20 miles across. They are lumpy, not round, and they look like potatoes with craters. To us on Mars, Deimos rises in the east and sets in the west. Phobos rises in the west and sets in the east. They move across the sky in opposite directions. I never got tired of watching one moon pass by the other.

Tonight, though, I wasn't on the telescope deck to moon-watch. I wanted to see the planet Earth.

I turned the controls and fine-tuned the focus.

There it was. A beautiful blue ball, streaked with swirling white as storms crossed the face of it. And behind it, the round white moon, bouncing the sunlight and redirecting it here to Mars.

I smiled sadly again. The 200 of us here on Mars were so far away. So alone in the vast solar system. To me, the Earth of DVD-gigaroms seemed so foreign but nice—a place of people laughing and crying and falling in love and having picnics in parks and watching the sunset behind mountains and crossing oceans and flying through the air on planes.

Because of the oxygen problem, I'd never have a chance to see any of that. Or any of the other incredible things about living on a planet that Mom says God designed to make the existence of humans possible.

I blinked and went back to the telescope. Thinking about what I'd never see, I wanted to cry. But I wouldn't allow myself to do it. Because out of all the people under this dome,

I was the only kid and used to being alone. I'd learned early not to cry, even when I felt like it. I'd learned early that I'd have to fend for myself. Other than my mom and Rawling, nobody in the colony paid much attention to me.

I stared at the Earth and the moon, hanging in the black of a universe that was so big no human mind could truly understand its size. I sat there a long time, thinking and wondering and feeling sad thoughts.

Then someone tapped my shoulder.

It scared me so badly that I would have jumped out of my wheelchair if my legs had worked.

"Relax, Tyce," Rawling said. "It's only me. I thought I'd find you here."

"Yeah," I said, my heart still pounding. "You did."

"Look," he said in a strange tone. "We've got to talk. It's about a secret your mom and I have kept from you for a long, long time."

CHAPTER 10

Below us, it was dim. Shadows darkened the rows of plants. The minidomes looked like black eggs rising from the ground. Only the hum of the electrical generators broke the silence. And too soon, when all the electricity died, there would be no noise at all.

"Outside the dome . . . ," Rawling started to say in a low voice. He had pulled a chair near the telescope and sat in it facing me directly so our eyes were at the same height. "What does it take for a human to survive outside the dome?"

"I thought you were going to tell me a—"

"Outside the dome," he said again, "what does it take for a human to survive?" He spoke firmly, like he was quizzing me and wasn't going to say another thing until I answered.

"With or without a covered platform buggy?" I asked. The Mars Project has two of them. These monstrous machines ride on huge rubber tires that don't sink in the Martian sand because gravity is less here than on Earth.

I've seen photos of cars, and platform buggies look nothing like them. The buggies are simply four wheels that support a deck. On the bottom of the deck are the electric engine and storage compartments. On the top is a miniature dome, similar in shape to an igloo, which covers the driver and passenger and can hold up to 10 people. A small tunnel sticks out from the minidome onto an open portion of the deck where a ladder almost reaches the ground. This tunnel has two entrances to allow people to get in and out of the platform buggy when it's on the surface of Mars. The outside entrance is sealed as someone steps from the inner entrance into the tunnel. Then the inner entrance is sealed before the outer entrance opens. In this way, little oxygen escapes the platform buggy's minidome. The big entrance of the space station's dome works this way too.

"Without," Rawling said. "You know how expensive the platform buggies are. They take a lot of room in cargo, cost millions to produce, and consume too much valuable energy when we run them. What does it take for a human to survive outside the dome without a platform buggy?"

"Humans need oxygen and water and protection from heat and cold."

"How do they get all that now?"

"Big bulky space suits," I said. "And whatever oxygen and water each person can carry."

He asked, "How long can a human last out there until he or she needs to return to the dome?"

"Supposedly a day," I said. "Only a day. But that's why we're here. To get the planet ready for humans to live outside the dome. So that later—"

"Later is 100 or 200 years away. Meanwhile, the entire planet needs to be explored."

"Do you really have a secret? Or are you doing this to me to keep me interested?"

Rawling didn't smile. "Machines. Robots. They don't need oxygen or water or heat. They don't take up a lot of cargo space on ships. For the cost of one platform buggy, you can have 100 robots. Robots are ideal, except for one thing." He paused. "Robots don't have human brains. A computer as big as a spaceship can't think and react the way a human can. So we can't begin to send robots out to explore the planet unless they are controlled by—and think like—humans. Are you with me so far?"

"Yes, but it hasn't been much of a secret. You said—"

"Tell me what you know about Earth labs that grow skin and bone for people."

"What does this have to do with—?"

"Tell me."

"Sure, I'll tell you," I said. "You and Mom made me study it as part of a school assignment."

"So you understand that 50 years ago, burn victims had no chance of healing their skin. But now doctors can take a piece of the victim's skin and grow it into big patches, just like growing a plant, then replace the damaged skin with the new skin."

"Yes, I know. Remember? You made me study it for three months as—"

"You know about replacement bones and replacement organs and how far that has come since the year 2000. And that doctors have learned how to grow biological plastics right inside the body. They have used steel and cable to rebuild joints. They've found ways to join all sorts of artificial materials to human body parts."

"Yes, yes, yes," I said, trying hard not to get impatient. "Come on. What's the secret?"

"Put it together," Rawling said slowly and quietly. "The need for robots with human brains, along with advances in medicine. Add one more thing. Then you'll have your secret."

CHAPTER 11

"One more thing," I repeated. "I don't get it."

"Virtual reality," Rawling said. "You've been in that robot simulation program two hours a day since you were eight years old. Tell me what you know about virtual reality."

"Well," I started slowly, "I put on the surround-sight helmet. It gives me a 3-D view of a scene on a computer program. The helmet is wired so when I turn my head, it directs the computer program to shift the scene as if I were there in real life. Or in the case of the robot training, it shifts to whatever video lens I want, giving me the chance to see in four directions, one direction at a time."

"Go on," Rawling said.

"Sounds come in like real sounds. Because I'm wearing a wired jacket and gloves, the arms and hands I see in my surround-sight picture move wherever I move my own arms and hands."

"Good," he said.

"Good? I'll bet any five-year-old Earth kid knows this stuff. What about this secr—?"

"Will you agree with me that the virtual-reality helmet and jacket are just extensions of your brain?"

He must have seen my puzzled look. He pointed at the telescope. "Just like this is an extension of your brain. You can't actually be on a moon of Jupiter, but the telescope lets your eyes go there, and your eyes show the moon to your brain."

"That's different," I said. "A moon of Jupiter is real. Virtual reality is just a computer program."

"Your brain doesn't know the difference. Not unless you tell your brain with your thoughts."

"Rawling," I said, "if you're trying to confuse me, it's working."

"Stick with me," he said. "This is important. Does your brain see?"

I thought about it. "No. My eyes see."

"You got it. Your eyes deliver information to your brain. When you look through the telescope, your optic nerves take the image and fire it into your brain. Your brain translates the information. But your brain doesn't see. It relies on the extensions of the brain. Your eyes. Your telescope. Or the extension of virtual reality."

I was beginning to understand.

"Your brain doesn't see anything," Rawling said. "It doesn't hear anything. It doesn't smell anything. It doesn't taste anything. It doesn't feel anything. Your brain is this incredible jumble of stuff packed into your skull that translates the information delivered to it by nerve endings. Some nerve endings are attached to the back of your eyes. Or to your ear canals. To sensors in your nose or on your tongue. To nerve endings in your skin and bones."

"In other words," I said, "you're telling me the body is like a virtual-reality suit wrapped around the brain."

"Exactly!" He smiled. "After all, it's like God designed an amazing 24-hour-a-day virtual-reality suit that moves on two legs, has two arms to pick things up, can feed and repair itself, and is equipped to give information through all five senses. Except instead of taking you through virtual reality, a made-up world, your body takes you through the real world."

"I never thought of it that way," I said. "But I'll agree with you. Now will you finally tell me the secret?"

"Soon," Rawling said. "But give me one more minute."

"One minute."

"It takes time for the brain to learn how to handle all the information delivered by the body," he said, excitedly falling into the teacher role. "For proof, all you need to do is watch a baby as it grows. Babies are clumsy and don't know how to work their bodies. Or how to understand the sights and sounds that their eyes and ears deliver to their new brains. But slowly, their brains figure out what information is being delivered, and babies begin to understand the world around them through the nerves of their eyes and ears and nose and tongue and skin."

"I know. I know," I said. "For my first two years in controlling a virtual-reality robot in the computer program, you always laughed and said that except for smelly diapers, I was just like a newborn baby."

"Because you were," Rawling said in a serious tone. "Your brain was learning to translate new information. Only this new information didn't come from your body but from the virtual-reality equipment, which was just like the extension of your body. You were clumsy at first, but quickly you got better until you now handle that virtual-reality robot just as if it were your own body. Learning those controls was like learning the controls of a complicated computer game." He took a deep breath. "So you're still with me after all that?"

"Yes."

Rawling took another deep breath. "Let me ask you this. If the information was delivered instantly, would it make a difference to your brain if the information reached it through eyes attached to your head, or eyes attached to a video lens a thousand miles or a million miles away?"

"It would," I said, after thinking about it for a few seconds. "Because your hands have to be near your eyes to pick something up."

"What if your hands were also a thousand miles or a million miles away?"

"Ha-ha," I said. "I know your secret. You're crazy. Like anybody could have arms a million miles long."

"I'm serious," he said. "It's the brain that matters and how it deals with the information. If your eyes, ears, and hands are just extensions of your brain, it doesn't matter how far away all those parts are, as long as two things are possible. First, these extensions instantly deliver information to the brain. And second, the brain is instantly able to direct the extensions. Will you agree with me?"

I looked at Rawling strangely. He was waiting as if my answer was very important.

"Well," I said, "I guess you're right. It wouldn't matter."

"If it doesn't matter, you could explore Mars. You could go out to the asteroids. You could see a moon of Jupiter. Not by telescope but by actually being there through extensions of your eyes and ears and the rest of your senses in the body of a robot. Would you like that?"

"You know I hate this wheelchair," I said. "But what you're talking about, that can't happen. It's only theory."

Rawling looked up through the dome at the stars. Then back at me. "It's no longer theory," he said softly. "It's you."

CHAPTER 12

"I promised your mother I wouldn't say anything else until we got together with her," Rawling said as he got out of his chair. "She's waiting for us in your minidome."

"You can't leave me hanging like this."

"It won't be long," he said. "Let me get you down there."

Normally, I didn't let anyone push my wheelchair. I mean, did other people ask for help when they walked? This time, though, I was too distracted, wondering about what Rawling had just told me.

Rawling wheeled me away from the telescope and took us down the catwalk to the second level. As he pushed me along the second level walkway, he grunted. "You must be getting heavier," he said. "I don't ever remember it being this difficult to move you around."

"Lack of oxygen," I said. "It's been getting tougher and tougher for me to wheel around too." But now I didn't care about that. I wanted to know more about the virtual-reality program. "Will you at least give me a hint about this robot stuff?"

"You won't have to wait long. Trust me, for as long as this secret has been inside you, another few minutes won't matter."

"Inside me?"

"Inside you. But I won't say another word until we meet your mother."

He kept pushing. When we reached the ramp, he guided me down to the main level. In another couple of minutes, we met my mother in our minidome.

"An X-ray," Rawling said as he handed me a big envelope. "An X-ray of your back and shoulders. From this afternoon's checkup."

I glanced up at him.

He sat in one chair on the other side of the minidome's common area. Mom sat on another.

"First of all," Rawling began, "you should know that we weren't going to tell you this until you were 18, the age of legal adulthood on Earth. A long time ago it was decided that when you reached that age, you would be given the choice to go ahead with the experiment or not. Except now, with the dome losing oxygen . . ."

He didn't have to finish for me. What he meant was that I wouldn't reach my 18th birthday.

"Anyway," he said, "look at the X-ray."

I did, opening the envelope and holding the sheet up to the light. The bones were gray-white against the darker film of the X-ray sheet. I could easily see the collar bones and shoulder blades and the top of my spinal column and the bottom of my skull.

"See where your neck is?" Rawling asked. "You'll have to look closely. See that short, dark rod, hardly thicker than a needle?"

I squinted at the X-ray and finally nodded. It was wedged directly into my spinal column at the bottom of my neck, just above the top of my shoulder blades. It looked like thousands of tiny hairs stuck out of the end of the needle into the middle of my spinal column.

"That's been there since you were a year old," Rawling said.

"What is it?" I asked. "How did it get there?"

Mom spoke very quietly. "It got there as part of an operation. I agreed to let them attach it to your spine. It was a very difficult decision, one I struggled with making. In the end, I felt I had no choice. I hope you will forgive me."

"Forgive you? But—"

"Tyce, it made things very hard here at the dome when we discovered I was going to have a baby. Everything for this project had been planned down to the last detail. You weren't one of those details. Director Steven was furious, but he couldn't send me back. They needed a plant biologist too badly to begin experimental work on hybrids for Mars. If I went back to Earth, with the time it takes to travel back and forth, it would put them years behind as they waited for a replacement. Director Steven threatened to send you back instead, as soon as you were born. But I knew the journey in a spaceship would kill you. Babies can't handle the stresses of g-forces and orbit shifts. So when he offered me a trade, I accepted it." Her gaze lowered to her hands.

"A trade?"

"Remember," she said, "I loved you too much to send you away and risk your death."

"A trade?" I asked again.

Mom hesitated. "Director Steven said everyone on the dome project needed to have a purpose," she finally answered, staring straight at me as if judging my reaction to her news. "Including you. So I agreed to the operation on your spine. The next ship brought in a neurosurgeon and all the experimental equipment needed. After the operation, the neurosurgeon went out on the next flight. He was paid six years' salary for all the time he spent in travel. But no one cared about the money, because it was decided that you could be the one to revolutionize space exploration."

"Me?" I said.

"As part of the long-term plan," Rawling said, "scientists had been hoping to use robots to explore Mars and do work that humans couldn't, based on virtual-reality extensions. The next stage in their experiments was to hook up the human nervous system directly into a robot's computer drive. They were hoping a human brain could control the robot."

In a flash, I understood why Rawling had always examined my back so closely during checkups. Why he'd been worried about my back after I fell out of the wheelchair the night before. Why he'd spent two hours a day since I was eight Earth years old, training me in the virtual-reality robot program. Why Mom and Rawling had made me learn everything possible about human implants.

"The needle in my back," I queried, holding up the X-ray against the light. "All those things at the end of the needle that look like fine hairs. Those are biological implants that have grown into my nerves."

Mom and Rawling nodded.

"Plastic fibers with a core that transmits tiny impulses of electricity," Rawling said. "You are the first person to get this implant. They hadn't planned on trying it in a human on Mars for at least another 10 years."

"Wow!" I couldn't keep excitement out of my voice. If I was right . . . "And the end of the needle coming out of my spinal column," I said, "it will attach directly to a computer input, right?"

Again they nodded.

"It will take a painless minor operation to cut open the skin and add an antenna plug to the needle," Rawling said. "It will barely stick out of your back."

"Double wow!" I said. Now everything Rawling had just talked about at the telescope made sense. The need for robots powered by human brains. Medical advances over the last 50 years. Virtual-reality extensions of the human brain. "You mean I can be hooked up to a robot?"

"If it works," Rawling said flatly. But he didn't seem happy. "Remember, no one has tried this before."

My mind raced. The senses of the robot will be an extension of my body! Just by using my brain, I'll be able to travel without my wheelchair! I'm going to be the one to revolutionize space exploration! The places I can go in a robot's body are limitless. I can . . .

Tears rolled down Mom's face.

"I don't get it," I said, puzzled. "This is great news. What's there to forgive you for?"

Mom didn't wipe away the tears. "Tyce, I've lied to you about one thing since you were old enough to talk . . . and it has pained me to do so. I have agonized over my decision ever since, wondering if I made the right one— letting my baby become an experiment. So here's the truth. You didn't lose the use of your legs because of the way you were born."

I stared at her. I didn't understand.

"It happened during the operation," she finished. "When the neurosurgeon inserted the rod into your spine, he accidentally cut some of the nerves that go to your legs."

CHAPTER 13

When Mom asked me to write this Mars journal, I thought it was going to be about living and dying under the dome. Instead, it has become learning about myself.

First of all, I'm scared. And it's been that way ever since two days ago, when I learned the truth about my handicap. At first I was excited about the thought of zooming around in a robot's body. But then reality settled in. This afternoon I'm going to be hooked up to the computer drive of a robot through the nerves of my spinal column. Rawling says it should work, but no one has ever tried it before. He says something might go wrong. It could do something to my brain if the electrical circuits haven't fused properly to my body with the biological plastic connections.

I say, what does it matter since I might die anyway from the oxygen problem in this dome?

I've also learned I'm crippled not from birth, as I've thought all these years, but because an experimental operation went wrong when I was a baby.

I don't know whether to be mad or sad about this. Or happy that I've got a chance to do something in space that no other person in history has been able to try.

Either way, it won't change the fact that my legs are useless.

I stopped typing at the keyboard. I reached for my red juggling balls from my wheelchair pouch and tossed them in the air. My hands automatically juggled while my brain thought. I needed to comfort myself with juggling because if I let myself think about what I didn't want to think about, I'd go crazy.

But here I was, beginning to consider what had made me cry all last night. I told myself to focus on the operation that crippled me instead.

In a way, I felt more sorry for Mom than I did for myself. She's the one who feels guilty over what happened because of the operation, although it isn't her fault. She didn't have much of a choice: Either she had to send me off to certain death on the spaceship or allow me to stay and become part of an experimental procedure. She'd only had a short time to make the decision—and all when my dad was out of communication range, so she had to make the choice on her own.

Maybe I should be mad at Director Steven, who forced Mom to make the choice. But he didn't plan on the operation going wrong. It did explain, though, why he always seemed to dislike me. Now I knew I reminded him of his terrible mistake in forcing me to be an experiment without any choice. At least that's what Rawling says.

It wouldn't do much good to get mad at Director Steven anyway, since it wouldn't change my situation. And I knew Director Steven had plenty of other problems now.

I stopped juggling and went back to writing.

Late the night I'd found out the real truth about my legs, one of the scientists went to Rawling with the committee's decisions—the committee Rawling had refused to join.

They call themselves the Life Group. They have 75 people, too many for security to arrest or fight. So they now have enough power to rule the dome. They say that unless Director Steven agrees to help them, they will do it themselves. They are trying to force him to make sure that 20 people die early so the other 180 will live. If Director Steven doesn't help them, they'll find a way to pick those 20 people themselves.

Then yesterday morning, Director Steven called another meeting for everyone under the dome. He said he didn't agree with the Life Group but was afraid a war would start if he didn't try to do something.

Director Steven said we had three days to figure out what was wrong with the generators. After that there would only be enough oxygen left for 180 people to survive until the ship arrived. He said at this point he felt he should see if any volunteers would give up their lives to help save the others if the generators did not get fixed.

It was very quiet when he asked for those volunteers.

I felt tears begin to roll down my cheeks again.

I mean, what would you do in the same situation? If you were going to die anyway when the oxygen was gone, would you volunteer to die early so you could save others? Or would you hope that others volunteered to die early so you could be saved?

I wish I could tell you what I decided about volunteering. But I wasn't given a chance. So I'll never know for sure, no matter what I tell myself.

Director Steven said some people wouldn't be allowed to be volunteers because of what they contributed to the long-term project. I was one of those people. He had learned through Rawling that I'd said yes to the experiment where the nerves of my spinal column would be attached to a robot's computer drive.

I forced myself to write in my journal what happened next.

Altogether, there were about a hundred people who would be allowed to volunteer to save the others. When he asked again for 20, nobody looked at anybody.

Then I heard a movement as some people stepped out of the back of the group.

Director Steven had asked for 20 volunteers, and 3 decided to give up their lives if the generator wasn't fixed in time.

I cried all last night. I haven't cried in years. But I couldn't help myself.

One of those volunteers was my mom.

CHAPTER 14

"Tyce, you know I believe God created humans with a body, a mind, and a soul. I know you can't prove the existence of a soul. You tell me that all the time. But you can't prove it doesn't exist." Mom stood beside my wheelchair in the part of the dome that overlooked the ferns and trees planted in straight rows. She had a hand on my shoulder.

"You're correct. No scientific instrument will measure or prove the existence of God or the soul," she continued. "But no scientific instrument can prove the existence of love or loneliness, either. Love exists. So does loneliness. You can feel it. And I believe your soul will be filled with one or the other."

"Please," I begged, "please change your mind about being one of the 20." I fought hard not to cry in front of her. It was bad enough when I did it alone.

"I know we've had these talks before," she stated, "but listen to me again. If we have souls, then there is more to this life than what we see with our human eyes. And there is someone beyond, waiting: God, who created us and this universe."

"Mom . . ." I couldn't help it. I began to cry.

She squatted beside me and stared into my face. She smoothed my hair as she spoke. "I love you. I love you so much it breaks my heart to think of leaving you behind. But my faith would be worth nothing if I could not face death bravely because of it. Our human lives are just a blink in eternity compared to God's promise of where my soul will fly after it leaves my body."

"No . . . ," I blubbered. "You can't. I don't want you to leave me behind."

Mom spoke very quietly. "I can't make you believe what I believe. I just hope that when you see how strongly I believe in God—even accepting death because of it—that my faith might lead you to believe in God too. If my sacrifice brings you home to God, then it'll be worth it. And I've already asked Rawling to take care of you when your father isn't here."

"All right," I said, tasting the salt of my tears. "I'll believe. I'll believe. If that's what it takes to save you, I'll believe anything. Just tell Director Steven you've changed your mind."

She stood again and looked out at the plants. "You know I can't do that. But don't give up so fast. We still have two days to find a way to fix the generators."

CHAPTER 15

"Your upper back giving you much pain?" Rawling asked.

"No," I said. "Can't feel a thing."

We were in the computer lab room. I was on my back on a narrow medical bed in the computer laboratory. I wore a snug, navy blue jumpsuit. My head was propped on a large pillow so the plug at the bottom of my neck didn't press on the bed. This plug was wired to an antenna that was sewn into the jumpsuit. Across the room was a receiver that would transmit signals between the body suit antenna and the computer drive of the robot. It worked just like the remote control of a television set, with two differences. Television remotes used infrared and were limited in distance. This receiver used X-ray waves and had a 100-mile range.

A half hour earlier, Rawling had frozen the area of skin

below my neck with a needle injection. It had taken him less than five minutes to find the rod in my spine and attach a computer plug to the end of it. With the plug sticking out, Rawling had stitched the small opening of my skin around the plug with careful, tight loops, explaining that if we weren't so short on time, we'd have waited a week for the skin to heal.

I didn't care about a few stitches that I couldn't feel anyway. I wanted to get started as soon as possible to see if this would work. My wheelchair was empty in the corner, and I hoped to keep the wheelchair empty for as long as possible. I'd dreamed my whole life about walking, and if it took my brain and a robot's body to do it, I was ready.

"I've got to go over this one more time," Rawling said. "I can't tell you enough how important it is."

"No problem. I'm ready," I said.

"Tyce . . . ," he warned.

"Um, ready to listen just one more time," I quickly finished.

"Good." Rawling began pulling straps tight across my legs to hold me snugly to the bed. "First, it won't be good if you move and break the connection. I doubt it will happen, since only your brain will be responding, and your brain, of course, cannot move. But this will be the first time anyone has ever done this, and I'd rather be safe than sorry."

He tightened the straps across my stomach and chest.

"Second, don't allow the robot to have contact with any electrical sources. Ever. Your spinal nerves are attached to the plug. Any electrical current going into or through the robot will scramble the X-ray waves so badly that the signals reaching your brain may do serious damage."

Rawling placed a blindfold over my eyes and strapped my head in position. Immediately, it began to itch under my chin.

"Lastly," he directed, "disengage instantly at the first warning of any damage to the robot's computer drive. Your brain circuits are working so closely with the computer circuits that any harm to the computer may spill over to harm your brain."

"Understood, understood, and understood," I said. I wanted to scratch myself under my chin. "I'm ready."

"No, you're not," Rawling answered. "Tell me how you're going to control the movements of the robot for me."

I spoke directly to the ceiling. My eyes were shut beneath the blindfold. "From all my years of training in a computer simulation program, my mind knows all the muscle moves I make to handle the virtual-reality controls. This is no different, except instead of actually moving my muscles, I imagine I'm moving the muscles. My brain will send the proper nerve impulses to the robot. It will move the way I made the robot move in the virtual-reality computer program."

"Correct," he said, sounding pleased. "It may feel strange at first, sending brain impulses in this way. Don't panic if it takes you some time to figure this out. Now, tell me when and how you disengage your mind from the robot controls."

My chin was driving me crazy. "If I see any object about to strike the robot's computer drive or if I feel the robot begin to fall or otherwise get close to danger, in my mind I shout *Stop!* The combination of throat and neck muscle movement from my brain impulses, plus the sound of that one single word, triggers the computer drive to disengage me instantly, and my brain awareness returns to my body here on the bed."

"Excellent," Rawling said. "Remember, this afternoon is just a test run back and forth in this laboratory. Nothing fancy or dangerous. Right?"

"Right."

"You know the blindfold is here to protect your real eyes from visual distractions. I also need to make sure your real ears can't hear anything. Any questions before I put the headphones on?"

"Just one," I said.

"Yes?"

"Could you please, please scratch under my chin?"

CHAPTER 16

In motionless darkness and silence, I had no sense of time. I knew Rawling would need to download the virtual-reality program into the robot's computer drive. But I couldn't guess exactly when this might happen.

As I waited, I pictured the robot. Its lower body was much like my wheelchair. Instead of a pair of legs, an axle connected two wheels. Just like a wheelchair, it turned by moving one wheel forward while the other remained motionless or moved backward. I knew I could handle direction changes easily. After all, in my real body, the use of spinning wheels was the only way I'd ever moved through the dome.

The robot's upper body was a short, thick hollow pole that stuck through the axle, with a heavy weight to counterbalance the arms and head. Within this weight was the battery that powered the robot, with wires running up inside the hollow pole.

At the upper end of the pole was a crosspiece to which arms were attached. They were able to swing freely without hitting the wheels. Like the rest of the robot, the arms and hands were made of titanium and jointed like human arms, with one difference. All the joints swiveled. The hands, elbows, and shoulder joints of the robot could rotate in a full circle as well as move up and down. The hands, too, were like human hands, but with only three fingers and a thumb instead of four fingers and a thumb.

Four video lenses at the top of the pole served as eyes. One faced forward, one backward, and one to each side.

Three tiny microphones, attached to the underside of the video lenses, played the role of ears, taking sound in. A speaker on the underside of the video lens that faced forward produced sound. This was the speaker that would allow me to make my voice heard.

The computer drive of the robot was well protected within the hollow titanium pole that served as the robot's upper body. Since it was mounted on shock absorbers, the robot could fall 10 feet without shaking the computer drive. It had a short antenna plug-in at the back of the pole to give and take X-ray signals.

I felt my heart beating fast in suspense. When was it

going to happen? When was the computer drive going to be ready? What would it be like? Would it work?

It seemed I waited forever in the darkness and silence of the blindfold and soundproof headphones.

I was just about to open my mouth and ask Rawling if there was a problem.

Then it happened. I began to fall off a high, invisible cliff into a deep, invisible hole. I kept falling and falling and falling. . . .

CHAPTER 17

"Tyce! Tyce! Tyce!"

In the blackness, my name echoed weirdly around me, as if I were trapped in a metal barrel.

"Tyce! Tyce! Tyce!" My name was so loud, it hurt.

I lifted my hands to my head to cover my ears. That movement seemed to rip the darkness off my eyes. I saw three blurry pairs of titanium hands waving wildly.

"Not so loud," I complained. Except my words came out slow and deep and warbly.

The three pairs of hands still waved wildly.

Then I realized I saw three pairs because I was using three eyes—the video lenses on each side and the forward lens.

I blinked a few times and concentrated straight ahead.

Much better. Now it was only one pair of wildly waving hands.

"Tyce!"

"Not so loud," I complained again in my robot voice.

I stared at my hands. Oops. My video lens zoomed in too close. A giant titanium knuckle filled my view.

I zoomed back. I saw the wall and bed and my body strapped on the bed. Weird!

My hands still waved. Finally I managed to get the focus right. Then I asked myself why I was doing something dumb like watching my hands work. Was I a little baby who had never seen fingers move before?

I thought about dropping my hands to my side and letting them rest there. Instantly, they moved where I wanted. This was great!

"Tyce!" It was Rawling. He had moved directly in front of me. My front lens saw his stomach.

Up, I mentally commanded myself.

The video lens tilted up.

I saw his face looking down on me. Blinking a few times to focus better, I saw his nose hairs. Too close. I backed out a bit. Then it was just right.

"You're too loud!" I said.

"It's not me," he said. "I'm whispering. You must be trying to hear too hard. Those speakers can pick up the sound of a feather landing on a floor. I'm turning them down."

I thought of listening less hard. The volume of his voice dropped. This was really fun.

"Rawling," I said, focusing on speaking properly. My voice became more normal. "How are you?"

"This is unbelievable," he said excitedly. "It's you in there!"

I blocked out my front view and switched to a side lens. It showed my body on the bed again. I zoomed in close. My chest rose and fell as the body breathed.

"Yes," I said, "it's me in here."

I kept watching the bed. It was very strange. That was my body on the bed, but it wasn't my body. My brain was working, controlling a robot's body. Very, very strange.

I switched to the rear video lens, then the other side, and then the front again. In a blur, it showed the back wall, the side wall, and Rawling's face.

Big mistake. Going in a circle that fast made me dizzy. I wouldn't do that again.

"Can you move?" Rawling asked.

In my mind, I pictured shoving back in my wheelchair.

Both robot wheels responded instantly. In a flash, I was going backward. Too fast!

Without thinking, I switched to the rear video lens.

The back wall was approaching too quickly.

Stop, I commanded the wheels. *Stop!*

In that instant, I fell into blackness again. Off that high, invisible cliff into that deep, invisible hole.

Just like that, I was back in my body. I felt the straps against my stomach and chest. I felt my itchy chin. And I heard a loud crash.

"Tyce!" Rawling shouted. "Are you all right?"

"Yeah," I said from the bed. I'd forgotten the stop command would disengage me from the computer drive. "But how's our robot?"

CHAPTER 18

Hello again, journal. I feel like a person in a cave who has just found enough gold to make him rich for the rest of his life, then watches as the cave entrance gets covered by a landslide. What good is the gold going to do then?

For me, the experiment with the robot was the best thing that ever happened to me. I had freedom for the first time in my life.

Rawling spent the rest of the afternoon with me. The robot wasn't damaged from smashing into the back wall, so we put it through dozens of trial runs. Each time I got a little better at using it. All the years in virtual-reality training have paid off for us.

I rested my fingers, thinking about what I'd write next.

The robot is amazing. It has heat sensors that detect infrared, so I can see in total darkness. The video lenses' telescoping is so powerful that I can recognize a person's face from five miles away. I can also zoom in close on something nearby and look at it as if using a microscope.

I can amplify hearing and pick up sounds at higher and lower levels than human hearing. The titanium has fibers wired into it that let me feel dust falling on it, if I want to concentrate on that miniscule of a level. It lets me speak easily, just as if I were using a microphone.

It can't smell or taste, but one of the fingers is wired to perform material testing. All I need are a couple specks of the material, and this finger will heat up, burn the material, and analyze the contents.

It's strong too. The titanium hands can grip a steel bar and bend it.

Did I mention it's fast? Those wheels will move three times faster than any human can sprint.

I love this robot. I can hardly wait to get back into it tomorrow.

All of this is the good news, just like finding gold.

The bad news is that we are one day closer to the dome running short of oxygen.

I finally have my freedom. And now I might lose it.

But worse—way worse—is the scary thought that Mom has volunteered to leave the dome so others can survive. I can't handle it. Life seems so unfair. I keep telling myself that somehow the solar panels will be fixed before tomorrow at noon.

Because that's when 20 people must get sent onto the surface of the planet to die.

CHAPTER 19

The next day, two hours before the deadline to have the solar panels fixed, Director Steven called another general meeting. It took me and Rawling away from our experiments with the robot.

All of us—director, dome techies, scientists, and me—met at the assembly area. Still in my wired jumpsuit, I sat near the front, since I wouldn't be able to see over anyone in my wheelchair.

This assembly was different than the others. Normally, Director Steven stood alone at the front on a small platform when he spoke. This time, the dome's five security guards, armed with stun guns, stood beside him. The guards were big men, their muscles like slabs of rock beneath their jumpsuits. In all the years of the Mars Project, they'd never been required to do actual police work. Today they looked very stern and serious.

Parked at the side were both of the dome's platform buggies. I fought tears since they were here for only one reason: to take my mom away.

She stood beside me. For once, I didn't care what other people thought. I reached out and held her hand. "Please don't go," I said. "Please."

"I love you, Tyce." She spoke quietly, but there was a tear in her eye. "Never forget that."

"Please don't—"

Director Steven began to speak, cutting me off. All the people behind me stopped their murmuring and shifting.

"I would say good morning," Director Steven said grimly, "but this is not a good morning. The final deadline approaches, and we've found no solution for the loss of oxygen. All seals to the dome have been checked. We're not leaking oxygen. We've taken apart the solar panels again and again, and we cannot determine why they fail to produce enough electricity to maintain oxygen levels. I now face the most difficult moment I've ever faced as director of the Mars Project."

He stopped to draw a breath. "These platform buggies will take some of us away from the dome. All radio contact between the platform buggies and the dome will cease. Those on the platform buggies will not be coming back. They will be heroes, making possible not only the lives of those who remain but moving the Mars Project forward. As you know, it's critical to keep it on schedule, because each extra year it takes to get the planet ready is an extra year that millions will starve on an overpopulated Earth. Because of that, the few who leave today will not only save the 180 who remain behind but the lives of millions of others. Those who leave on these platform buggies will be remembered for their sacrifice for as long as mankind exists."

He looked at Mom and smiled sadly, then addressed the rest of the crowd. "As you know, we've had a few volunteers agree to leave the dome. However, we'll need to remove at least 20 people for there to be enough oxygen for the others to survive until the ship arrives. For that reason, I've drawn names."

Immediate angry shouting rose like thunder around me.

Director Steven put up his arms in a request for quiet. It took several minutes.

He spoke again. His face appeared weary, unlike the cocky director who such a short time ago had insisted I leave his office. "Do any of you see another way? We cannot permit everyone to die. Better a few should die than all of us."

More shouting. Again he raised his arms. This time it took even longer for him to be able to speak.

"Understand two things. First, the security guards have been instructed to enforce this order. Their guns are set on stun. If your name is drawn, and you refuse to go, you'll be placed on the platform buggy by force. Please don't make this more difficult on all of us."

The shouting grew even louder and longer. Now it didn't make a difference that Director Steven held his hands high and pleaded for silence.

Finally he stepped down from the platform and headed toward one of the platform buggies. In the roar of the shouting, he climbed the buggy's ladder. When he reached the deck and turned around to face us below, the shouting stopped as people tried to figure out why he was there.

"Second," he said, "my own name is on top of the list. I will not ask anyone to do anything I cannot do myself."

These words were greeted with shock. Director Steven had volunteered. How could anyone else refuse if his or her name was drawn?

Mom stepped forward.

"No!" I cried. "Don't go!"

She turned around. Tears ran down her face, but she smiled. "Tyce, more than anything I want you to choose to believe in God—to realize that life beyond the body is more important than anything else, and that, with God waiting in heaven for you, you don't have to fear death."

Mom left me and slowly moved to the ladder that led up to the platform buggy deck. She began to climb. Away from me. And toward her own death.

To think of Mom giving up her life to save me and the

others of the dome was to understand a love that felt like a sword piercing my heart. To think of her gone made me so empty that I almost couldn't breathe.

In that moment, I understood a bit of what she'd been trying to tell me all along. There was something inside me that no scientific instrument could measure or explain. Had I really been created by a God who cared—for me?

Without realizing that my arms had moved, I felt the rims of my wheels in the palms of my hands. Without saying a word, I pushed forward in my wheelchair to the platform buggy. If Mom trusted in God, then I too would trust that my soul had a place to go.

She heard the sounds of my wheels squeaking. She turned. Shock filled her face. "No!"

"Yes," I said. "I don't care if I'm needed for the robot experiments. If you go, I go."

We were whispering because it was deathly still. With everyone watching us, not a single voice spoke.

Mom pivoted and looked up at Director Steven on the platform buggy deck. "Make him stay behind," she begged. "Have the guards stun him so he cannot follow. I am trading my life for his."

More heartbeats of silence.

Director Steven checked the sheet of paper in his hand. "I cannot let him stay behind. When I drew names, I did not set anyone apart. Because of that, his name is on this list too."

CHAPTER 20

We slowly traveled across the Martian landscape, 10 of us
in one platform buggy and 10 in the other, following closely
behind. Except for me and Director Steven, two security
guards, and the two techies who first volunteered to leave the
dome, the rest were scientists.

After the entire list had been read, Rawling had tried
to volunteer. He had said there were too many important
scientists, too many of the best brains in the solar system
about to die. Rawling had said it wasn't right, and he should
at least be allowed to take the place of one of those scientists.
Director Steven had said that the decisions had been made
and the names drawn in all fairness. We were to proceed
accordingly.

One of the security guards whose name had been drawn

tried to make a run for it, but he was stun-blasted by two others and hauled up into the platform buggy.

Just like me. Only I wasn't hauled up because I had been trying to get away. Without the use of my legs, I couldn't climb. So a big security guard had thrown me over his shoulder like a sack and carried me up the ladder. Another security guard had brought up my wheelchair. Not that it made a difference. There wasn't much room to move around in the platform buggy observation deck. The doors weren't locked, but with no space suits and an atmosphere of carbon dioxide waiting outside, there was no place to go.

All of that had taken place a half hour earlier.

Now we were at least 20 miles clear of the dome. The inside of our platform buggy was very quiet, except for the humming of the electric motor that powered the monstrous wheels beneath us.

At one end of the buggy, Mom sat, hugging her knees. A security guard was at the steering wheel. The other seven scientists were scattered in different groups, whispering among themselves. Director Steven was driving the other platform buggy, with the nine other people for passengers.

As for me, I was beside Mom, in my wheelchair by the window. I let my hands mindlessly juggle the red balls as I stared out at the landscape.

The sun began to drop behind the distant mountains. Our dome was on a valley plain. Towering above the nearby hills, those mountains, black and jagged and awesome against the sun, stood 50,000 feet high.

I've been told that sunsets on Earth can be incredible. A mixture of reds, oranges, and pinks all streak across the sky.

Not so on Mars. Since there's so little atmosphere, there are few particles of dust or smoke to work as prisms to change the sun's light into different colors as the sun nears the horizon. Here, the sun always looks like a blue ball of fire.

What's incredible, however, are the pinks and reds and roses of the land itself. With its red soil and the salmon color of the sky, the beauty of the desolate landscape is haunting and sad.

Of course, part of the reason I felt that way as I looked through the clear bubble of the platform buggy was a result of seeing where all of us were headed. Director Steven said he didn't want the others back at the dome to be reminded of what would happen to us. So we'd have to travel out of sight of the dome and then park, waiting for our oxygen to run out.

CHAPTER 21

The strangest thing happened the next morning.

I woke up. Alive.

Mom had prayed for us the night before, because we both expected that the oxygen in the platform buggy would run out during the night. Usually only two or three people went out in it at a time, so it did not carry enough oxygen for all of us for a long period. We expected to go to sleep and never wake up.

As I blinked and rubbed my eyes, I saw surprise on the other faces as well.

We didn't have a chance to wonder about it for long.

"Good morning, everyone." Director Steven's voice came over the communication speaker, talking to us from the other platform buggy. "Please make sure you have breakfast. I want all of you to remain as healthy as possible."

I gave Mom a strange look. She gave me a strange look.

Wearing the jumpsuit I'd fallen asleep in, I rolled over on the floor and pulled myself into my wheelchair.

"To those of you who are surprised to be breathing this morning," his cheerful voice continued, "please let me apologize for yesterday's drama. I assure you that neither platform buggy will run short of oxygen until the supply ship arrives from Earth."

I pushed over to the window, fighting to move the wheels as I'd been doing over the last few weeks. As I stared across the space between the platform buggies I could see into the other platform buggy where Director Steven was facing the microphone.

"Let me explain," Director Steven said calmly. "The oxygen level in the dome is far lower than anyone knew. Had I been truthful about it, there would have been panic and civil war as people fought for the remaining oxygen tanks. After I did all the calculations, I discovered there was only enough oxygen for 20 people to survive."

He cleared his throat. "That left a simple problem. How could I get those 20 out of the dome without the other 180 fighting to go? You have probably guessed by now how I came to a simple solution. I made it appear as if these 20 were the ones who would die. That way, no one would stop them from leaving. And you, of course, are the 20. Mercifully, the others left in the dome will not face the fear that comes with knowing the oxygen will run short. They will just become sleepy and die peacefully."

What? I thought wildly.

"The few of you who volunteered to give up your lives are here because you deserve to live. The rest of you are among the greatest scientific minds in the solar system. I made a decision that you must be spared to continue the Mars Project."

What?

Director Steven glanced across the short space between the platform buggies. He caught me staring at him in surprise. "You too, Tyce," Director Steven said. Surprisingly, he smiled at me. "We cannot afford to lose you. Not after what you proved yesterday."

A hundred and eighty people had been condemned to die just to save the few of us?

"Rest assured, people," Director Steven finished in his smooth voice, "we do have enough oxygen. The tanks that were taken a few nights ago were hidden on these platform buggies. The two men who assisted in that task are the two security guards among us. In fact, one even pretended to resist entering the platform buggy, just to make it look more realistic that we were headed for death. Of course, no one else in the dome knows any of this. But those of us in the platform buggies will survive. None of you should feel guilt, as this was my decision and you had no choice in the matter."

The speakers in our platform buggy clicked off as Director Steven hung up his microphone.

Back at the dome, time and air were running out for everyone. Including Rawling, the one man I trusted above everybody else.

CHAPTER 22

On the other side of our platform buggy, the security guard was handing out nutri tubes for breakfast.

I struggled to push my wheelchair over there. It had been getting more and more difficult to move. I wondered if Director Steven had lied to us about the oxygen, just so we'd die peacefully and without fear.

When I reached the security guard, he gave me my choice of scrambled eggs and bacon or scrambled eggs and sausage.

"Like there's a difference," I said.

He grinned. "Good point." He was square-shouldered, with a crew cut and a squashed nose, as if it had once been broken. "Scissors?" he asked.

"No, thank you," I said. As usual, I just ripped open the top of the tube.

"Hey, muscles," he teased, laughing, "promise you won't get mad at me."

"Ha-ha," I said. I pushed away and found a spot near the edge of the observation deck. If breakfast had to taste bad, at least I could eat it where I had a nice view.

I'd slept for nearly 10 hours, and the sun was already above the horizon, casting long shadows from the jagged rocks that littered the Martian sand.

Then it hit me. If the reason I struggled to push my wheelchair was because of lack of oxygen, how come I could still rip open a nutri tube?

I thought back over the last few days. Not once had I been forced to use scissors on the nutri tubes. So maybe it wasn't my hands and arms getting weak. But why then was it still difficult to push my wheelchair?

I thought about that as I slowly chewed and swallowed the gooey yellow paste that was called scrambled eggs and bacon.

Mom moved beside me and sat on the floor to eat her breakfast. "I'm still in shock," she said. "Director Steven had this planned out for a long time. Early enough to steal the oxygen tanks and pretend he knew nothing about it."

"Yeah," I said, my mind on my wheelchair.

"I'm curious what you think," Mom said thoughtfully. "Is what he did right? I mean, Director Steven—"

"Can you help me out of my wheelchair?" I asked, interrupting her.

"Sure, but—"

"Now?" I asked. I gave her what was left of my nutri tube.

Mom set it aside and lifted me out of the chair by grabbing under my armpits. She set me on the floor.

I leaned my back against the glass of the platform buggy wall. "Thanks."

"Tyce?" she asked. "What is it?"

I spun the back of the wheelchair toward me. There was a small tool kit underneath the seat that made it possible to take the wheelchair apart and put it back together. "Give me one minute," I said, reaching for the tool kit. "I'll tell you if I'm right about something." I tilted the wheelchair on its side, then undid the bolt that attached the wheel to the axle and took the wheel off.

The other scientists were in their own discussions and didn't pay much attention. After all, they were the greatest minds in the solar system. To them I was just a kid. A crippled kid.

With the wheel in my lap, I used a screwdriver to dig out the bearings that let the wheel turn on the axle. I tried to spin the bearings. They hardly moved. That, at least, explained why it had been so hard to move my wheelchair. And that also explained why the solar panels would not work properly.

Suddenly I knew, without a shadow of a doubt, what the problem was!

I put the wheelchair together as quickly as I could, had Mom help me back into my wheelchair, and then approached the security guard.

CHAPTER 23

"Director Steven," I pleaded, "you have to let them know."

I was at the console of our platform buggy, speaking into my headset. Director Steven sat at the console of his platform buggy, also wearing a headset. I'd just finished telling him about what had happened to my wheelchair and the ball bearings. They'd been ground down, probably by the microscopic silicon of Martian sand, making them hard to move. What if the wheels on the solar panels had the same problem?

He looked across at me. The platform buggies were parked side by side in the shade of a hill. "No," he said, meeting my eyes directly.

"No?"

"They already believe we're dead. It'll cause panic if they find out we're still alive."

"But this can save them!" I said.

"You aren't sure of that."

"No, but—" I was talking in a low voice. The security guard who had set me up at the console was standing at the opposite wall because I'd asked him if I could have a private conversation with Director Steven.

"But nothing." Director Steven ran his hands through his hair. "Already their oxygen levels are dangerously low. Even if they fixed the panels now, the generators wouldn't produce enough oxygen to save them."

"We could drive back," I begged. "We could share our oxygen with them as they wait for the generators to make more oxygen."

"I will not gamble these 20 lives on another wild guess of yours," Director Steven said. "If you're wrong and we go back and share our oxygen, we too will die. It's that simple."

"But—"

"But nothing. We sit here and wait. There will be no communication with the dome. Am I clear?"

"But—"

"Am I clear?"

I pulled off my headset and smiled.

The security guard came back to the console and took the headset from me. "Well?" he asked. "Did you get what you wanted?"

"Sure did," I said. I reached for the switch that would

link our platform buggy radio with the main radio back at the dome. I flipped it on as if there was no question about it.

The security guard frowned. "I didn't think there was supposed to be any communication with home base," he said.

"I just talked to Director Steven about it," I said. Which was true.

I leaned forward and spoke clearly into the radio microphone. "Platform buggy one to home base. Tell Rawling McTigre to talk to Tyce. Platform buggy one to home base. Tell Rawling McTigre to talk to Tyce. Platform buggy one to home base. Tell Rawling—"

"Grab that kid!" It was Director Steven shouting into the speaker of his platform buggy, his voice echoing in ours. "Shut him up! Now!"

The security guard pulled me away so quickly that I almost fell out of my wheelchair.

Director Steven stood at the glass wall of his platform buggy, glaring at me. All other eyes in both platform buggies stared at me.

"Sit him in a corner and make sure he doesn't move." Director Steven's voice was thick with rage. "If he tries anything else, put him outside. Without a space suit."

CHAPTER 24

It took five minutes for the scientists in our platform buggy to forget about me and Director Steven's threat.

Mom drew up a chair beside my wheelchair. "What was all that about?"

"I wish I had time to explain," I said, "but I need to go to sleep as fast as possible."

"Tyce?"

"Can you trust me on this? I need to sit here with my eyes closed. Turn my wheelchair around so no one can see my face. Make sure nobody comes by and disturbs me. That's all I ask."

"For how long?"

"Until I wake up," I said. "Please?"

Mom sighed. "This is so strange."

"So is letting all those people die."

Without a word, she turned me away from the other people in the buggy. My view was of the back side of the hill. Rock and sand in all colors of brown and red and black.

I closed my eyes and waited in the wired jumpsuit I was still wearing from when I left the dome. I hoped that someone at the dome had heard my short message. I hoped that Rawling would understand what I meant. I hoped that very soon, in the darkness of my mind, I would fall off the edge of a high, invisible cliff into a deep, invisible hole.

"Tyce?"

"Took you long enough," I said to Rawling.

I tilted my video head and peered into his face. His skin was gray, and he was sweating badly. I clicked around the room—slowly, to keep from getting dizzy—with my other three video lenses to see if anyone else was with us.

"Someone heard your broadcast and called me in my minidome," he said. "I tried to radio the platform buggy, but I didn't get an answer. If you wanted me to turn on the robot, why not say so instead of making me figure it out?"

"Because," I answered, spinning my robot wheels back and forth, warming up, "then Director Steven would have known how I intended to talk to you. And he would have stopped me."

Rawling wiped his face. His jumpsuit was blotched with sweat. "You guys are supposed to be dead."

"Long story." I looked around the lab and found the tools I needed. I handed them to Rawling. "I will tell you after. But we need to get to the solar panels."

"Sure," he said, "but I don't feel so good. Maybe we can get someone else to help you."

I reached across and pinched his shinbone with my titanium fingers.

"Ouch!" Rawling said, shocked.

"You have got to stay awake. The lack of oxygen is starting to get to you."

"Lack of oxygen? But—"

"You do not have much time. Follow me." I wheeled to the door of the lab. I tried twisting the knob with my fingers. I twisted too hard. It fell off in my hand. "Oops. I do not know my own strength."

I wheeled back, picked up a chair with both hands, and held it in front of me. I crashed into the door with it. The door popped open. Checking behind me with my rear lens, I made sure Rawling was following me. He staggered slightly as he tried to keep up.

"It is the wheels of the solar panels," I explained quickly. "The panels work fine. But if the railing wheels are stuck even slightly, the panels cannot track the sun's movement as they slide along the roof of the dome. They do not have the right angle to catch enough sunlight to produce power."

I noticed no one was walking around the dome. "Where is everybody?" I asked.

"I think sleeping," he said. "Which is what I want to do."

Continuing forward, I reached back with one arm. I grabbed Rawling's hand.

"Ouch," he said again.

I didn't let go. "You are coming with me." I led him up the ramp to the second-floor walkway, then along the walkway. Soon we were at the ladders that reached up to the solar panels.

"You will have to climb," I said. "I cannot. All you need to do is disconnect two or three wheels from the solar panel railing. Bring them back down."

Rawling nodded slowly.

As I waited below, I scanned the dome. No movement anywhere. Were people already dying?

I switched to infrared and scanned the nearest minidome. The minidome itself was a light red, showing that it held slightly more heat than the cool air of the dome. Inside, a deep glowing red in the form of a body showed me where someone rested on the bed. I watched carefully and saw a slight rising and falling of the form. The person was still breathing.

Switching off infrared, I went to the visual light spectrum, seeing colors as normally viewed by human eyes. I changed video lenses to see Rawling. He was nearly finished taking off a couple of wheels.

I hoped I was right in my guess.

If I was wrong, I'd be in my robot body, helpless to prevent all these people from dying over the next few hours.

CHAPTER 25

I opened my eyes in the platform buggy.

There was noise and excitement behind me.

I spun in my wheelchair.

Everyone was gathered at the far window, staring down from the platform buggy at the desert floor.

I smiled. I knew what had their attention.

I wheeled up beside them. "It's a robot," I said loudly.

My words quieted them down.

One of the scientists frowned at me. "Of course it's a robot. We aren't stupid. We want to know what it's doing here. Five minutes ago, I saw it coming here at a speed I estimated to be 24 miles an hour. Then suddenly it stopped in front of our platform buggies. And what's that in its hands?"

"Solar panel wheels," I said. "Damaged solar panel

wheels. I'm not totally sure it's from microscopic particles of Martian sand, but that's my best guess. I think over the years, the sand has seeped into the dome. My wheelchair can hardly move because the ball bearings have been ground down, and the only reason I can come up with is sand."

I had everyone's attention.

"The solar panels follow the sun," I said. "If the wheels on the solar panel railings have the tiniest bit of drag, the solar panels will always be a few degrees behind the best angle to catch maximum sun. I think that's what's been happening. Slowly, the generators have been dying. Not because anything is wrong with the panels. But because something's wrong with the wheels."

"What's the discussion in there?" Director Steven asked from the other platform buggy.

"Mom, could you turn the speaker down and let me finish? Then all of you can decide what to do."

"I'll turn it down," another scientist volunteered. "This is all so crazy. There must be some truth in it."

"Thank you," I said. It hurt my head to look up at everybody from my wheelchair. "That robot brought back a few of the wheels from the dome to prove that's the problem. We need to return to the dome. We can replace the wheels and begin generating electricity within hours. The people in there don't have to die."

From the corner of my eye, I saw Director Steven waving, trying to get our attention.

I ignored him and explained more. "The oxygen levels in the dome are so low that everyone has passed out. They need oxygen from the platform buggy reserves to survive until the generators kick in again. It'll take about an hour to return. That's just enough time to save them."

"And if you're wrong," another scientist said, "we'll have given them the oxygen that would keep us alive."

"That's why I brought back the solar panel wheels," I said. "To prove it to you."

A third scientist snorted through his thick white beard. "You brought them back? That's a robot out there. You've been here in your wheelchair, asleep. Now I understand why Director Steven thinks you're dangerous. You've lost your mind."

I'd forgotten. The experiments with the robot were so recent that only Mom, Rawling, and the director knew about them.

I grinned at all the people staring at me. "I think I have a way to prove to you that I'm in control of the robot."

CHAPTER 26

It had become a beautiful sensation, falling off the edge of a high, invisible cliff into a deep, invisible hole.

When the falling ended, I focused my video lens upward at the platform buggy observation deck. I saw nine people crowded at the glass wall, peering down on me. Behind them, I knew, my motionless body sat in my wheelchair.

The heat of the Martian sun seemed to glow in my titanium bones. It was midday, and the temperature registered 65 degrees Fahrenheit. In my entire life, I'd never been outside. It felt as marvelous now as it had when I'd first left the dome to scoot across the plains.

And wind. It whistled across the stark rocks embedded in the sand. Tiny bits of sand rattled off my wheels and arms as I sped across the landscape. It was such a glorious feeling of being alive.

I wanted to sit where I was and enjoy all of this—the things that humans on Earth can have anytime, just by stepping outside. But I'd made a promise to the scientists in the platform buggy. And they, in return, had made a promise to me.

If I could convince them I was the brains of this robot, they'd follow me back to the dome and share their oxygen with the others.

First I raised one titanium hand and waved.

They hadn't expected this. I could see on their faces that a few were startled. Others waved back, smiling.

I waved at Director Steven in the other dome.

He crossed his arms and frowned at me.

I stopped waving. My left hand held two solar panel wheels, small like the wheels of roller blades on Earth. I dropped my right hand, which held one wheel, down to the ground. Holding the wheel tight between two fingers, I dragged my other titanium finger as I began to move the robot back and forth.

When I was finished, I surveyed my handwriting in the sand. Take us home, it said in big letters.

I looked up again and saw that many were pointing down. They could see it clearly, and they understood.

But that wasn't all I'd promised as proof.

I turned the robot to face them as they watched me from the observatory decks of both platform buggies.

In my mind, I took a deep breath. Breathing was one of the few things I did better in my own crippled body than I did in the robot body. Still, just thinking of breathing helped me concentrate. I wanted to do this right. I wanted to be able to lead them to the dome across the packed sand of the desert that let this robot run like it was a leopard.

All eyes were on me as I began to deliver on my promise to them.

I switched the small solar panel wheel from my right hand into my left hand, so my left hand held all three wheels. Then I tossed one of the small solar panel wheels in the air with my left hand. I caught it with my right, but as I was catching that wheel, I tossed the second wheel from my left hand into the air. A split second later, I tossed the third wheel.

And just like that, I was juggling.

CHAPTER 27

We did it. We made it back to the dome just in time.

All of us worked together to fix the solar panels and give oxygen to the people who were on the verge of slipping away.

I was right. Microscopic sand particles were the problem. It had taken years, but eventually the buildup of sand and the wearing down of the ball bearings had made the solar panel wheels drag just slightly—enough to throw off the panel angles. So now that the ball bearings have been fixed, there's no longer a danger of anyone dying from lack of oxygen.

After the immediate threat of death was gone,

the people turned their attention elsewhere . . . to Director Steven.

Everybody under the dome is angry at him. And who can blame them? In the same way that he used my body as an experiment by forcing my mom to let a surgeon put a rod in my spine, Director Steven used all of the techies and workers as pieces of a puzzle, shifting them around to suit what he thought the Mars Project needed. Whether he was right or wrong, the dome scientists disagree.

But the fact is, no one trusts him now so he's under guard in a small lab. Soon the next supply ship will arrive. When it leaves to return to Earth, he'll be shipped back with it. Rawling has been voted in as the new director.

I feel sorry for ex-Director Steven. He faced a difficult decision in trying to choose who should live and who should die. But I think that was just it. He made the decision without talking to anyone, as if he were trying to be God.

After facing death, learning how I really became crippled, and seeing my mom's willingness to sacrifice her life for me, I'm a lot more open about that subject too.

The subject of God.

Mom has always said faith is a sure hope in things unseen. I've decided that just because I can't find a way to measure the existence of God, it doesn't mean he isn't there. And it's the same thing with the soul.

Actually, all of this has helped me stop feeling sorry for myself in my wheelchair. I've realized something. All of us, even the best athletes, are imprisoned by our bodies. Against our will, our bodies will someday grow old or sick. And, sadly, our bodies will die.

When I think of it that way, I'm in the same prison you are. Sure, in an uncrippled body, your prison cell might be bigger and brighter but not by much. You can run at eight miles an hour, and I can roll along in my wheelchair at only three miles an hour, and in my robot body I can go three times as fast as you. But all of those speeds are so tiny compared to the vastness of the universe that it doesn't matter at all who's faster.

What I've begun to understand is that, although we're stuck in our bodies, we can have freedom of the soul. I'm going to give this a lot more thought.

Anyway, I've got to shut down this computer and go. Rawling—I mean, Director Rawling—is yelling to me about someone seeing aliens outside the dome.

Ha. Aliens. Not very likely.

But Rawling is insisting I get into the robot body and do a quick search.

I'm excited about getting outside on the surface of Mars again, but I'm not expecting to find anything. Everybody knows there aren't any aliens on Mars.

Right?

JOURNAL
TWO

CHAPTER 1

Ahead of me, somewhere in the jungle of tall, green bamboo corn, a man's life depended on how quickly I could reach him.

This was no virtual-reality computer simulation program, like the ones I'd practiced for years in the science lab. It was the real thing. I'd been given so little time to get ready that all I knew were the basic facts about my mission.

The man's name was Timothy Neilson. He was a high-level medical techie—a technician who helped the scientists carry out their experiments. His job was to tend what we called the cornfield, a large patch located in a greenhouse outside the dome. Neilson's emergency beeper had gone off 15 minutes earlier, and it was a good thing I had already been in a practice rescue session, hooked up to the robot I was now controlling. That meant I could roll into action immediately.

But I didn't know if that was fast enough. Timothy Neilson wasn't responding to radio communications, even though the computer link showed that his receiver and transmitter were both in perfect working order.

I knew one other thing about Timothy Neilson. The emergency signal reaching the dome from a computer chip embedded in his space suit told us the suit was leaking oxygen and heat so badly that he now had less than 10 minutes to live. If he was still alive.

The gigantic black shell of the dome was five minutes behind me across a stretch of red desert sand. That meant I'd have to find Timothy Neilson in five minutes and get him back to the dome in the remaining five minutes.

Two things would help me. First, I held a GPS that allowed me to track the location of the signal chip in his space suit. Also, as I neared his body, I could switch to infra-red vision and look for the heat escaping his space suit.

Even with the GPS and infrared to help me, however, I was in trouble because of the bamboo corn stretching high in all directions around me.

Although this was Mars, the stuff around me truly was as thick as any jungle. My mother is one of the scientists who has worked hard for 14 years to genetically alter Earth plants to survive on the surface of Mars. None can—so far—but these hybrids came the closest. The stems of the plants were tall and thin and strong like bamboo plants, with wide, long leaves like those of corn plants. The entire field—a half-mile square of rows and rows of bamboo corn—was enclosed by a huge greenhouse tent of clear, space-tech plastic sheeting that gave the plants the protection they needed to survive.

With 100-mile-an-hour sandstorms that covered half the planet and an average temperature of minus 20 degrees Fahrenheit, life on Mars wasn't easy. But my mom believed the next generation of these plants would be able to grow without the greenhouse. In addition to the oxygen given off by the plants, the Mars Project would begin pumping oxygen into the atmosphere. Eventually, scientists hoped humans would be able to live on Mars without being under the protection of the dome. And that would help solve one of Earth's problems in the 21st century—overcrowding.

I was somewhere in the middle of this field, with four minutes remaining to find Timothy Neilson.

Using my robot wheels, I rolled down a path between two rows of bamboo corn. The leaves tickled like silk against my titanium shell. Above the rustling of those leaves, I heard the whistling of Martian wind as it found tiny gaps in the greenhouse tent. Unlike the dome, this wasn't sealed perfectly. It didn't need to be—the plan was to see if these plants could thrive with only some protection. If they lived, their seeds would be crossbred and genetically changed again to make the next generation even hardier. I listened as the wind whistled and sand rattled against the plastic. . . .

No! I told myself I did not hear what I thought I was hearing: movement in the corn leaves, just out of sight. Like the noise of dozens of creatures slipping away among the stalks of bamboo corn.

I swiveled the robot body, scanning around me. Only the silent, tall green stems surrounded me like prison bars.

Then I saw a darting movement. But it came and went so quickly that I told myself it was just my imagination. Aliens, I told myself firmly, do not exist.

I pushed forward, wondering if those nonexistent creatures were about to attack me.

My GPS chirped. Loudly. I would have jumped if I hadn't been on wheels. It chirped louder and louder, telling me I was getting close to Neilson.

Suddenly I came to broken plants, pushed over and sideways as if a man had crashed into them at a full run. I swerved and followed the crooked path.

It was easy to see footprints in the soil where the weight of the man's feet had crushed the wide leaves at the base of the stems. I rolled forward. It was like tracking an animal that had run in complete panic, not caring what it hit as it fled.

As I followed a twisting path through the bamboo corn, I had no choice but to believe something I did not want to believe. Someone—or something—had chased Timothy Neilson.

Impossible, I told myself again. This was Mars. The scientists claimed there was nothing alive on this planet that could hurt us.

I scanned in all directions, but the bamboo corn made it impossible to see beyond the reach of my titanium arms.

I switched to infrared vision, which let me see heat instead of light. The green outlines of the stems and leaves against the pink light of the sky disappeared. In infrared vision, I saw a blur of warm orange (the plants) standing on a deeper, brighter orange (the warmer sun-soaked soil), surrounded by a very light orange color (the cooler air).

Beyond the warm orange of the plants, I tried to sense the red shapes of living creatures.

Then I told myself I was dumb. Even if aliens did exist, which I knew was impossible, why should I expect them to have the same kind of body heat as humans?

The chirping of the GPS guided me ahead. I rushed as quickly as I could.

Seconds later, my infrared located the red outline of a space suit that was bleeding body heat.

Timothy Neilson.

"Are you all right?" I asked in my deep robot voice.

No answer.

I switched back to normal vision and focused on the white fabric of his space suit. He was lying on his stomach, his legs twisted beneath him where he had fallen in the middle of the bamboo corn. His space helmet was hidden by the leaves that had fallen on top of him.

I scooped him into my arms, grateful for the strength of titanium limbs. Without hesitation, I wheeled back toward the dome.

I now had 6 minutes and 25 seconds to get Timothy Neilson to medical help. If he was still alive. If I wasn't attacked by whatever had attacked him.

Because if I could trust my eyes, it looked like teeth and claws had ripped the holes in his space suit.

CHAPTER 2

"How is he?" I asked Rawling. Of anyone under the dome, he was my best friend. He was a mixture of father and buddy and teacher. I've always said I could ask him about anything, and I knew he'd treat my question with respect and honesty.

I was now disconnected from my robot body and back in my wheelchair, trapped by my useless legs. I sat in front of Rawling's desk in his new director's office.

"All Neilson's vital signs are fine," Rawling said in answer to my question. "The med techs tell me he's in a coma. He landed hard on his head and gave himself a concussion. If he comes out of it—" He stopped himself and sighed. "When he comes out of it, they expect he won't suffer any permanent brain damage from lack of oxygen. It looks like you got him back in time."

"Good," I said.

Rawling studied me with curiosity on his face. "All right, Tyce Sanders," he finally said after watching me. "I want to hear all of it."

I should have known he'd figure out I'd kept something secret. Best friend or not, Rawling knew me almost better than anyone else, including my own father, whom I only saw every three years. "How did you guess?" I asked.

"It wasn't a guess," Rawling said dryly. "A man doesn't rip his own space suit to shreds. Maybe falling down a cliff with jagged rocks would have done it. But it couldn't have happened out there alone in the cornfield. There has to be more to it than what you told the med techs."

"I told the med techs the truth about what I saw," I said. "But what I didn't say is that I wonder if he really was alone."

Rawling raised an eyebrow.

I described everything I could to him. The twisted path that Timothy Neilson had crashed through in the bamboo corn. The big stretches between footsteps that showed he'd been running. And the sounds of creatures scampering among the leaves.

"That makes sense," Rawling said. "I don't want to believe it, but it makes sense."

Now it was my turn to raise an eyebrow. I was getting better at it. I'd sit in front of a mirror and work on raising one eyebrow, then the other. I practiced it because I liked the way it looked when Rawling did it. "It makes sense?" I asked.

"I'll explain in a minute," he said. "First, tell me why you decided not to tell the med techs."

"You're the director," I stated bluntly. "If there is something out there, I figured you should be the one to decide whether you want anyone else under the dome to know about it—in case people start to panic."

"From worrying about an alien attack?" Rawling queried.

"That would be big news for all of us," I responded. "Wondering what was out there and waiting. I mean, you saw what happened to Timothy Neilson's space suit."

"Just his space suit, right?" he asked. "I know what the med techs told me, but I want to hear it straight from you."

All of a sudden I realized that Rawling was talking as if there actually were aliens. Goosebumps chilled my neck. "His body looked fine to me. So if they only hurt his space suit, maybe I showed up before they could finish the attack." I stopped and thought about what I'd said. "Whatever they are."

Rawling began to fiddle with a pencil on his desk. He spun it several times and spoke as he stared at it. "To find out there is other life in the universe besides life on Earth would be one of the most incredible discoveries in scientific history. Then to find out that this alien life-form will attack humans . . ." He spun the pencil a few more times. "You know our last director kept too many secrets from people under the dome."

I nodded. Those secrets were another part of why ex-director Steven was heading for Earth on the next spaceship leaving Mars.

"Wrong as he was to decide who should live and who should die when the dome was running out of oxygen, he has some of my sympathy. Sitting behind this desk is not easy. Neither are some of the decisions." He rubbed his face. "Conditions back on Earth are not the greatest. Because of overpopulation, governments are barely maintaining control as everyone fights for water and other resources."

"Yes," I said. I wondered why he was telling me something I already knew. Something everybody on Earth knew too.

"What I'm saying," Rawling told me, his voice heavy, "is that if news of aliens—especially aliens that attack humans—reaches Earth, it might cause riots."

"I understand that," I said. "Are you telling me there are aliens, and you've kept it a secret?"

"I'm telling you that if I do keep it a secret, people here might get hurt. If I keep it a secret, I'm doing exactly what the former director did. And I don't know if that's right." He sighed. "But on the other hand, if I call an assembly and tell everyone what I know, eventually word will get back to Earth and billions of people may panic."

I cleared my throat. "What exactly do you know?"

Rawling didn't answer. Instead, he flicked on his computer. The monitor on the edge of his desk lit up. I saw the cursor move across the screen.

"Here's why what you told me makes sense," he said, opening a file.

It wasn't a text file or a video file but an audio file. A short clip of excited shouting.

I didn't hear it right the first time. Or at least, I didn't want to believe I had heard it right.

"That voice belongs to Timothy Neilson," Rawling said. "It's his last radio communication back to the base. I've ordered the radio operator to keep it quiet until I can figure out what to do about it." He replayed the audio clip for me.

"Help!" Timothy Neilson's terrified voice shouted from the computer. "Help! They're chasing me! Dozens of them! Help me! Help me! Help—"

All that followed those words of panic was static.

I stared at Rawling. Rawling stared at me.

"To make matters worse," Rawling said, "we're expecting the spaceship late tonight, with dozens of newcomers to the base."

CHAPTER 3

Some of you on Earth might already know about me. I'm the kid on Mars who was writing a journal about the final days under the dome, when it looked like everyone here would die.

Even if you didn't read the long e-book of that journal sent by satellite back to Earth, you can probably guess that everything turned out fine in the end. Otherwise, I wouldn't still be writing, would I?

So why this new e-book, starting today, June 26, AD 2039?

Mom figures anyone my age might be interested in a Mars journal, so as part of my ongoing homework, she's making me add to the first journal. If you feel sorry for me because you don't like

to write, either, I'll thank you now. I wasn't happy
with being forced to do it.

"Tyce, are you cleaning up your room?"

It was Mom, calling me from the common living space in
the middle of our tiny minidome.

"No," I called back. "I'm at the computer. Doing homework. Remember? The homework you gave me?"

I guess if there's one good thing about writing my journals, it's this: an excuse to avoid other things, like cleaning
my room.

"All right, all right." I heard her laugh. "Can you wrap it
up soon? I need to give you a haircut."

Like that was a good reason to hurry up and finish. I'd
almost rather get poked by a needle than squirm under a
sheet while she clips my hair and comes dangerously close
to clipping my ears. And let's just say her haircuts are not
a work of art. She's a scientist, not a stylist. Worse, because
we can't waste water under the dome, we're only permitted
showers twice a month. The rest of the time we use an evapo-
rating deodorant soap. My next scheduled shower wasn't for
another week. If she gave me a haircut tonight, I wouldn't
be able to wash the itchy hair off my neck and shoulders
until then.

"Haircut?" I hollered. "I just had one!"

"It was three months ago," she said in an amused voice.

"No way! It's been only six weeks! I sure don't need one this soon."

Mom walked through the entrance into my room. With hands on her hips, she did her best to look stern. "Don't lie. Three months. I marked it on the calendar because I knew you'd try to get out of it."

"I wasn't lying," I protested weakly. It figured as a scientist she'd keep track. "It was six weeks. Mars time." Here on Mars it took 687 days to circle the sun. Which meant a Mars year was about 1.9 times longer than on Earth. So my six weeks' Mars time and her three months' Earth time were about the same.

"Very funny," she said, unable to hide a smile.

"Wow," I said. "You look great."

"Don't change the subject." She smiled again.

"It's true," I said. "You do look great."

Normally, Mom didn't care much what she looked like, but tonight her hair was done nicely. I could smell perfume, and she wore a dress I hadn't seen her wear since . . .

"I get it," I said. "Dad's coming home."

"Exactly. In about four hours. Which is why you're going to clean your room. And after that I'm giving you a haircut."

I pointed at my computer.

"Yes, yes. Finish what you were writing."

"Mom . . ."

In my mind, I heard Timothy Neilson's voice as Rawling

replayed the audio. "Help! They're chasing me! Dozens of them! Help me! Help me! Help—"

"Yes?" Mom asked when I didn't finish my thought.

I really wanted to tell her about the aliens. Rawling had said I could if I wanted, because he trusted her, above all others under the dome, to keep the secret too. But she looked so happy about my father coming home that I didn't want to worry her.

"Nothing," I said, turning back toward my keyboard. Now I didn't feel like writing in my journal anymore. "Give me a few minutes to clean my room, and I'll be ready for my haircut." I forced a smile.

Clipped ears, in comparison to alien monsters that chased humans, suddenly didn't seem like such a bad thing.

CHAPTER 4

Four hours later, I was among those waiting outside the dome
on the platform buggy to watch the landing. The other platform buggy sat beside us, empty except for the driver. The
pilots, crew, and new project members would go back to the
dome in that one.

I strained my eyes, looking upward. There was tension
among us. While no previous landing had failed, there was
always the potential for disaster. If anything went wrong, my
father could die. Then the rest of us. Slowly. Because we were
in the early stages of the Mars Project, the spaceship was our
only lifeline to Earth. It had all the supplies we needed to survive another three years.

I reached down to the pouch hanging from the armrest
of my wheelchair and pulled out three red juggling balls.

Although it was dark, I began to juggle, keeping all three in the air without even thinking about what I was doing.

After five minutes, people began pointing upward. I let the juggling balls fall back into my lap and stared at the sky through the clear roof of the platform buggy's minidome.

At first, it looked like a star growing brighter among the millions of stars in the Mars night sky. It wasn't a star, though. NASA called it the Habitat Lander.

The whole journey from Earth was complicated. My father and the rest had taken a Crew Transfer Vehicle from Earth, about a six-month trip through space. Waiting for them in orbit around Mars was the Habitat Lander. They hooked up with it and switched ships. Rawling had once explained it to me in Earth terms. It was as if they were crossing an ocean. They came over in a big ship, and once they reached harbor, a little tugboat took them the final distance to shore.

But there was a difference. The journey had to be carefully planned so it occurred when Earth and Mars were nearest each other—roughly 50 million miles apart. At any other time, their orbits placed the planets up to double or triple the distance apart. And little tugboats on Earth didn't have to deal with the intense heat of Martian atmosphere.

The bright light I now saw was the result of the Habitat Lander moving downward so quickly that, even in the sparse atmosphere of Mars, its bullet-shaped heat shield glowed with friction.

I held my breath as I continued to watch. There was silence around me in the platform buggy as everyone else did the same. We all knew this was not a simple tugboat operation.

Coming in at too steep an angle would fry everyone aboard. Coming in at too shallow an angle would bounce them off the atmosphere toward Jupiter, without enough fuel to allow them to reverse and try again.

Although the Habitat Lander moved quickly, it seemed painfully slow to us down on the Martian surface. This was partly because it was still so far above us and partly because of our fear and worry.

Up there, my father was rolling the Habitat Lander to the right or left as it blazed through the upper atmosphere, steering it like an out-of-control sled careening down the steepest snow-covered mountain. Soon—too soon—he'd have to find a way to stop it.

The Habitat Lander's glowing heat shield, now appearing bigger than the sun, suddenly dropped straight down. I gasped. My eyes followed as it flipped and tumbled, a blaze of fire heading directly toward distant mountain peaks. Then the blaze became shattered jewels of fire as it exploded on contact.

I took another deep breath, reminding myself of what I already knew but so easily forgot because this was only the second landing I'd witnessed. That blaze was only the heat shield, discarded and dropped as part of the landing process. I let out a sigh of relief and searched the dark sky for what needed to happen next.

Retro-rockets.

Somewhere up there, if the Habitat Lander was still fine after dropping the heat shield, parachutes would have been released from the nose of the craft so it could land—feetfirst. Very soon, retro-rockets would kick in to help the braking process.

I found myself holding my breath again. One . . . two . . . three . . .

Like a mushroom of flame, the retro-rockets burst into sight, maybe a mile above us. The burst drew our eyes like fireworks, and all of us on the platform buggy focused on it, following it downward.

I had my eyes open, but in my mind I was praying—talking with God. Some people might think he wasn't there to listen, but I had faith that he was. It was hard-earned faith too. It came when I thought I'd die during the dome's oxygen crisis. When the crisis was over and I had time to think about it, I realized that when you get pushed to the edge of life and begin to wonder what's on the other side, your heart is really and finally open to believing God is behind this universe. You begin to understand that he's as invisible and as strong as love.

Finally the outline of the Habitat Lander appeared

above the brightness. The retro-rockets pushed hard against gravity, and slowly the Habitat Lander settled on the surface of the planet. The parachutes sagged downward, covering the top of the space vehicle.

Cheers and whistles filled the platform buggy. They had made it safely.

Soon I would see my father. For the first time in three years. Because his job was so important to him.

I couldn't help but wonder if he would be just another alien visitor.

CHAPTER 5

As we drove up to the dome, the outer door opened to allow both platform buggies inside the tunnel. When the buggies moved inside, the warm, moist, oxygen-filled air from the tunnel instantly turned into white, ghostly vapor and escaped into the cold Martian atmosphere. The inner door, of course, was still sealed to keep the dome's air from escaping.

As soon as both platform buggies had entered the tunnel side by side, the outer door shut behind us. Only when it was completely sealed against the atmosphere would the inner door be opened.

While we waited, people in our platform buggy waved at the newcomers in the other platform buggy. I tried to pick out my father, but I couldn't. Too many people were standing in front of me. While a wheelchair is great because it always gives you a place to sit, the disadvantage is no different from being seated at a baseball game with everyone standing in front of you to watch a big play.

We had to wait patiently as a demagnetizing process cleared both platform buggies of Martian dust. We had to wait longer until the sealing process of the outer door was complete and both platform buggies had rolled into the dome. Then the inner door began to close and seal behind us, so both doors now protected us from any air leaks to the Martian surface.

I was the first one off the platform buggy, lowered in my wheelchair with ropes by people on the platform.

Mom was waiting for me. She stood beside me as other people poured out from both platform buggies and climbed down the ladders to the surface of the dome.

Finally, among the last people, my father appeared. He climbed down slowly. After the weightlessness of space, even the weak gravity of Mars took some adjustments.

It gave me time to study him. In one way, it was like watching an interesting stranger. In another way, it was like looking at myself. I was growing tall, just like he was. Mom would often point to his photo and comment that I was also beginning to look like him. I had dark blond hair like he did. My nose and jaws and forehead were bigger than I wanted them to be, and I hoped the rest of my face would catch up so I would look more like him. My father was big, like a football player. I would be heavier and bigger too, if my legs didn't weigh next to nothing.

Mom stayed by me, her hand on my shoulder, as we waited.

I knew she was happy to see him. I knew she wanted to run forward. But it was nice she didn't abandon me. Unlike my father always does, I couldn't help but think, by always going off into space.

He turned and scanned the crowd. I could tell the instant he saw my mother. A big grin crossed his face, and he broke into an awkward half-run. He threw his arms around Mom, and they hugged and kissed.

I turned my head. I mean, what kid wants to see his parents smooching?

Then something—or rather someone—caught my eye as I looked away from my parents' hugging and kissing.

The last person, back toward me, was climbing down the steps of the other platform buggy. Except it wasn't just a person. It looked like a kid about my age. I could hardly believe it. I'd spent my entire life alone around adults. Now there was finally someone my age!

The hugging and kissing continued beside me. My eyes, however, were riveted on the new kid. What would he be like? Would we be friends? Was he hooked on astronomy like I was? Wouldn't it be cool to be able to share the stuff I was doing with a robot body?

I kept staring. The kid had short, black, straight hair. He was kind of skinny in the standard space uniform of a blue jumpsuit.

Finally, the kid reached the ground. He turned toward me. Except he wasn't a he.

He was a beautiful she. With dark eyes and high cheekbones. Asian—and beautiful. (Had I said that already? The beautiful part?)

And when she smiled and her eyes met mine across the short distance between us, I gulped.

Wow.

CHAPTER 6

Was I ready to pursue aliens?

Yes; so ready that I got up early the next morning, though I usually hated mornings because I had a habit of staying up too late at the dome telescope.

After the arrival of the Habitat Lander, my parents had walked around the dome, talking for hours. I hadn't heard them come in because I was asleep, just like they were now, in the room on the opposite side of the minidome.

In my own room, I was up and restless because of what Director Rawling McTigre had decided yesterday. He intended to delay his announcement about the alien monsters for 48 hours. In that time, he hoped I might be able to find out more details, enough so no one would panic about the situation.

That meant that in about an hour, Rawling would send me back into the experimental bamboo corn to search for the truth about the aliens. It was something I thought might be interesting to add to my journal.

I fired up my computer, rested the keyboard in my lap, and began to describe everything I knew about Timothy Neilson and his run-in with the aliens.

"Tyce? Tyce?"

I'd been so used to hearing my mom's voice interrupting me that it took a second to figure out that the male voice coming from the other side of the minidome was my father's.

I saved my computer file and shut the machine down before I wheeled out into the common living area.

He was standing there in jeans and a T-shirt. He needed a shave. He held a nutri tube in one hand, a mug of coffee in the other. "Did you get a chance to open the present I got you?" he asked.

"The CD with the top 100 rock songs of the 1900s?" I said. That was his music, not mine. Ancient stuff. "Looks great. Thanks."

"We can listen to it together," my father said.

"Yeah. Thanks." I tapped my fingers on the arm of my wheelchair.

He sipped his coffee. "Anyway, how are you?"

"Fine," I replied.

"Got time to share some breakfast?" My father made

a face. "Not that this artificial stuff comes close to a real breakfast."

"Wish I could," I said quickly, "but I've got to go."

"This early? Where?"

"Places. Maybe I'll tell you later, if I can."

He frowned. "What's the big secret?"

"Got to go," I said as I wheeled my way past him. I didn't care if he thought I was rude. After all, he'd been gone for three years. He'd be on Mars for only another few months until the orbit was in position for a return trip to Earth. And now he expected me to drop everything for him?

Not likely.

I had some aliens to catch.

CHAPTER 7

"Ready for those aliens?" Rawling asked, smiling.

"Which one would you like me to go after first?" I asked. "A slimy green one? Or a fat purple one?"

"Help out all earthling kids," he said. "Get Barney."

"Huh? Barney?"

"You know, the fat purple one," Rawling said, then stopped. "Sorry. Forgot you weren't brought up on Earth. You see, there was this television show where . . . and now I remember. It was a dinosaur . . . and it had been around forever . . . but it could have been an alien . . . and . . ." Catching my puzzled expression, he shook his head in disgust at himself. "Forget I even mentioned it. We've got serious business ahead of us."

We did.

As usual for all robot work, we were in the computer lab. As usual, I was on my back on a narrow medical bed, plugged into a receiver for the 100-mile range of X-ray waves.

"Let's go through the checklist," Rawling said. "I know. I know. We've been through this before," he said as I rolled my eyes. "But just like flying, safety is the first matter of importance."

With Rawling I knew better than to argue.

He began pulling straps across my legs to hold me tightly to the bed so I wouldn't accidentally jump and break the connection between the antenna plug in my spine and the receiver across the room.

"First," Rawling said, "don't allow the robot to have contact with any electrical sources. Ever. Your spinal nerves are attached to the plug. Any electrical current going into or through the robot will scramble the X-ray waves so badly that the signals reaching your own brain may do serious damage."

Rawling tightened the straps across my stomach and chest. "Second, disengage instantly at the first warning of any damage to the robot's computer drive. Your brain circuits are working so closely with the computer circuits that any harm to the computer may spill over to harm your brain." He placed a blindfold over my eyes and strapped my head in position.

"Understood and understood," I said.

"Lastly," he said, "is the robot battery at full power?"

"Yes. And unplugged from the electrical source that charges it."

The robot was at the far end of the dome near the entrance. Since the receiver worked at a distance, it wasn't necessary to keep the robot nearby. Before coming to the lab, I'd made sure the robot was ready for use.

"Good, good," Rawling said, squeezing my shoulder. "Any last questions before I soundproof you?"

"No," I said confidently.

"You're looking forward to this, aren't you?"

It was dark for me under the blindfold, but I grinned as if I could see Rawling's face. "Big-time," I said. The robot was a freedom that made up for my crippled body. No one else could wander the planet like I could.

"Then let's go." He placed a soundproof headset on my ears. The fewer distractions to reach my brain in my real body, the better.

It was dark and silent while I waited for a sensation of entering the robot computer.

My wait did not take long. Soon I began to fall off a high, invisible cliff into a deep, invisible hole.

I kept falling and falling and falling. . . .

CHAPTER 8

It never failed to amaze me. As I lay on the bed in the computer lab, light patterns from the other end of the dome entered one of the robot's four video lenses. Translated digitally into electrical impulses, that light followed the electronic circuitry into the robot's computer drive. From there, the electrical impulses were translated into X-ray waves that traveled through the dome to the receiver in the computer lab. From the receiver, the waves beamed to the wires in my jumpsuit, which were connected to the antenna plug in my spine. As the electrical impulses moved up the nerves of my spinal column into my brain, my brain did what it always did when light entered my real eyes and hit the optical nerves that reached into my brain—it translated the light patterns at the far end of the dome into images I could recognize. A similar process also allowed the robot to hear—but through sound waves that reached my own ear canals.

No differently than thinking about moving one of my own arms, I thought about moving the robot arms. And immediately it happened. I brought my titanium hands up in front of a video lens and flexed my fingers, wiggling them to make sure everything worked properly.

That's when the sound waves of a female voice entered the robot speakers and instantly entered my own brain. Actually, it was more like the sound waves of a female scream.

I switched to my rear video lens and saw the image of a female jumping backward. It was her. The girl I had seen last night was standing a few feet away from me. Evidently she'd recovered quickly from the scare of meeting the robot; she now stared with open curiosity.

As a robot, I was about her height. My video lens looked directly into her face. From this close distance, I saw her eyes were brown. She wore tiny silver cross earrings. I rolled my wheels forward a few inches and backward a few inches.

She jumped again.

"Greetings, earthling," I said. The robot's voice box worked like a telephone. Although it was capable of sounding exactly like my own voice, words tended to come out more mechanically. In speaking to this girl in front of me, I dragged out my words and talked in a nasal tone, just like I'd heard fake robots talk in science fiction movies I'd downloaded onto my computer. I don't know why I decided to do this. It must be because I have a weird sense of humor and she was too new to the dome to know this robot was actually hooked up to a person.

"You can talk?" she said, surprised.

"Yes, earthling. I can do many simple things. I can add two plus two. It equals four. Am I right?" I kept talking in that nasal, fake robot voice.

"Yes!" she said. "What about eight times eight?"

"Sixty-four. Did you not know yourself such simple mathematics?"

"Of course," she said, folding her arms. "I was just testing you."

"Testing? What is testing?" I asked. This was fun.

"I guess if you had real brains you'd know, wouldn't you?" she replied smugly.

Ouch. I deserved that.

She stepped closer and looked me up and down. The robot body was ugly, all right, but in her eyes probably better than the crippled body of a kid her age. "What's your name?" she asked, smiling. She tilted her body left and rested her right hand on her right hip.

I had to think quickly. I'd never thought of the robot having a name. I didn't want to give her mine. It might be fun to keep secret as long as possible the fact that I was directing the robot from my real body. "Bruce," I said, grabbing the first name that came into my mind.

"Bruce?" She smiled again. I liked that smile. "How did you get a name like that?"

"From my mother," I said in a weird, slow robot voice. *From my mother?* What kind of dumb answer was that? If I had robot legs, I'd have kicked myself.

She laughed. "Ask a dumb question, get a dumb answer. My name is Ashley." She stuck out her right hand. "It's nice to meet you."

I shook her hand with my titanium one, careful not to squeeze too hard. "Nice to meet you too."

"Well, could you give me a tour of the dome?"

I could get to know her as the robot, and she wouldn't have to stare at my crippled body in my wheelchair. That didn't sound too bad. "Later, please, earthling. When I return."

"Where are you going?" she asked, confusion on her face.

"To save all other earthlings," I said. "It should not take me long." I wheeled away and headed toward the dome entrance.

She waved good-bye, giggling—probably at how stupid I was.

CHAPTER 9

I wheeled outside the dome to a Martian sunrise.

I've been told that the sky on Earth is blue and the rising sun is yellow, with clouds around it colored pink, red, and orange. I've also been told that in the middle of the day, clouds are white, or if they hold rain, gray.

Not here on Mars. The sun is blue against a butterscotch-colored sky. Later in the day the sky becomes red as sunlight scatters through dust particles at a different angle. At this hour, wispy blue clouds hung high in the butterscotch sky, but they'd disappear as the day became warmer.

Now, this early, it was cold—about minus 100 degrees Fahrenheit. A 60-mile-an-hour wind hit me, but it didn't have much force because the Martian atmosphere is so thin. Some blowing sand rattled against my titanium shell.

Once out of the dome, I felt free. I didn't have to wear a space suit. The cold and lack of oxygen didn't hurt my robot body. Best of all, my crippled legs no longer mattered. I was able to wheel across hard-packed sand toward the cornfield at the speed of a galloping horse.

Which I did.

Five minutes later, I stopped in front of the huge plastic-sheeted greenhouse.

Rawling and I had decided that the first thing I should do was check for holes in the sheeting. The greenhouse was designed to trap sunlight and heat. It was not designed to be sealed against the Martian atmosphere, so we expected that somewhere, along the miles of plastic sheeting, there might be a rip or 2 or 12.

Slowly I made my way around the outside of the greenhouse. I wasn't just looking for rips, though. I was looking for a place where aliens might have entered.

And 15 minutes later, I found it. More correctly speaking, I found tracks.

The hole itself was a couple of feet high and a couple of feet wide. It didn't have the smoothness of a rip. By zooming in with my video lens, I clearly saw scratches, as if a claw had been used to tear the clear plastic sheeting.

The sand below this hole was packed harder than the sand on either side. In the softer sand at the edges of this packed path, a few tracks were visible. The wind had begun to fill in the tracks with drifting sand, but I could still see enough to know the tracks were not my imagination.

They were about the size of the palm of my hand—my real hand, not my robot hand—and about half an inch deep. I could not make out any more details, however, because the sand had drifted.

I did know two things for certain: The tracks were not human. And they led into the cornfield.

I spun back and followed the plastic walls of the greenhouse tent until I reached the same entrance I'd used when rescuing Timothy Neilson. The same entrance he'd taken when he went inside to check the growth levels of the plants, unaware that minutes later he'd be desperately calling for help.

It was much warmer in the greenhouse. Unlike the rest of the planet, there was enough oxygen in here from the plants to hold heat. That, combined with the greenhouse effect and the heat of the soil, made it above freezing. Not that I cared one way or another. I was well protected by my robot body.

I rolled inside, scanning in all directions. As before, the tall bamboo corn blocked my view. While these plants did need some water and the protection of the greenhouse, they practically thrived in the Martian air.

You see, while the atmosphere of Earth is 21 percent oxygen, 78 percent nitrogen, and 1 percent argon and carbon dioxide, the atmosphere of Mars is 95 percent carbon dioxide, 3 percent nitrogen, and 2 percent argon and other gases. Humans breathe in oxygen and exhale carbon dioxide. Plants do the opposite, which is very handy. So plants give us what we need, and we give them what they need.

Since Mars is already rich in carbon dioxide, the plants only needed water to survive. And since Mars is such a dry planet, the plants were genetically designed to need very little of it. Any moisture they received was sprayed through nozzles from narrow plastic tubing that ran in grids along the ceiling of the greenhouse tent.

Because I could see so little, I followed the rows of bamboo corn to the hole in the plastic sheeting. It didn't help much. On the outside, there was a packed path. On the inside, the path disappeared, as if the alien creatures had scattered in different directions once they had entered.

That left me with too many questions.

Why had they entered?

Where did they go once inside?

Were they still inside?

Where did they go after they left, if indeed they had left the greenhouse?

Where had they come from?

And the most important question of all: Why had they attacked a human?

I wasn't worried about what would happen to me if they

attacked my robot body. First of all, my titanium shell was a lot stronger than human skin and bones. Second, even if they were able to somehow damage my robot body, I could leave the robot almost instantly. In my mind, all I needed to do was shout *Stop!*

From the greenhouse wall, I decided to push into the bamboo corn and try to follow one set of blurred tracks.

I pushed aside stems of bamboo corn. My wheels rolled over other stems. I switched to my rear video lens and saw I was making a clear path through the plants. It was a straight path, unlike the one Timothy Neilson had made in his panicked run.

I realized something else. My path was the only path.

Yet I was almost certain that some kind of creature had ripped a hole through the plastic sheeting of the greenhouse tent. I was almost certain that many of those creatures had entered the greenhouse tent. But where were the bent and trampled bamboo-corn plants that showed their paths?

The only answer I could come up with was that these creatures were small enough to move among the plant stems instead of plowing over them, like my robot body did.

But if they were that small, why had they frightened Timothy Neilson? Every person chosen for the Mars Project had passed dozens of tests. People didn't make it to Mars if they were wimps or cowards. Had the creatures frightened Timothy because he simply hadn't expected any other kind of life-form? And how and why had they managed to do so much damage to his space suit?

I followed farther into the bamboo corn. I came to a spot where water from the nozzles at the ceiling had worn a small gully in the soil between the stems. Tracks littered the edge of this little depression. There was no water, of course. Even in the greenhouse, any water that didn't soak into the soil for the plants quickly evaporated.

A sound drew my attention away from the tracks at the edge of the gully. A scurrying sound. Then more scurrying. I saw nothing because of the bamboo corn that surrounded me, but the scurrying got louder.

I switched to infrared vision. As with the last time I was in the greenhouse, I saw the different shades of orange that reflected the slight heat of the plants and soil. Unlike the time I'd rescued Timothy, however, I saw shapes of deep red, the shapes of something alive.

Aliens!

Dozens of them!

Closing in on me from all directions!

I switched back to visual mode and saw only bamboo corn.

Back to infrared. I was about to be swarmed. Any second these aliens would break through the screen of bamboo corn that hid them from me.

I heard a click. A hiss.

I strained to hear. There seemed to be hundreds of the clicking sounds. The hissing became a roar in my sensitive hearing.

As the moving red shapes leaped all around me, I switched to visual again. I saw the darkness of moving objects in the air. Without thinking about it, I brought my titanium hands up to protect myself. I felt solid contact.

In the same instant, cold hit me.

And in the next instant, my brain seemed to explode. It felt like I had run into a wall at full speed in total darkness.

Without warning, I began to fall . . . fall . . . fall. . . .

CHAPTER 10

I awoke to see Rawling staring down at me with concern on his face. "Hello," I said with a croak.

"Glad you're back."

"Back?" I struggled to sit up. I realized I wasn't wearing my blindfold or the soundproofing headset. Nor was I strapped to the bed. "Back?" I repeated. "Where did I go?"

"That's what I'm trying to figure out," Rawling said. "Your body didn't go anywhere, but you were out for 6 minutes and 10 seconds."

"What?" I replied, startled.

"The computer shows the exact time that you disconnected from the robot body. Just over six minutes ago. Your body on the bed jerked around as if you had been shocked by electricity. You didn't make contact with any electrical sources, did you?"

Slowly, I remembered my last moments in the robot body. Clicking. Hissing. Dark objects in the air. Sudden cold. The sensation of hitting a wall at full speed in total darkness. "Not that I know of. Not unless I was hit by aliens with electrical currents in their bodies."

As I told Rawling what I'd experienced, he listened gravely. Then he said, "It's a possibility. If they are alien life-forms, they might well contain strong electrical or magnetic forces. We just don't know."

Rawling helped me sit up. "The good news is, you have a clean bill of health. Your pupils aren't dilated. Blood pressure is fine. Heartbeat is normal. Brain waves are fine."

"We'll need the robot body to figure out what happened," I said.

"Sure. But it wouldn't be right to send anyone in there. Timothy Neilson was attacked by those things, and it took a robot to get him out. And now it looks like they were able to take down an indestructible robot body. If aliens managed to stop it, how much chance do we have to survive an attack?" He took a deep, deep breath. "Here's the problem. We really need to know what those aliens are and what they're capable of doing. But I can't let anyone go out there if we don't know those things. And we won't know those things if nobody can go out there."

This was not good.

CHAPTER 11

After a very quiet and quick nutri-tube supper a few hours later, I decided to leave the minidome. My father and I weren't talking much. Mom seemed mad at both of us because we weren't getting along like she wanted. It was just easier to leave. It seemed weird in there, because my parents were so into each other. It wasn't that I was jealous or anything. Really. The guy goes away for three years, but when he comes back, he's the king. Me? I was suddenly useless and out of place. They had each other. All I had was a robot that I'd just named Bruce, and poor Bruce was stuck in the middle of a cornfield.

I decided to go where I usually went in my wheelchair when I wanted to be alone. To the telescope, far above the rest of the dome.

It took me less than five minutes to reach the telescope. I rolled into place where the dome astronomer usually sat and punched my password into the computer control pad.

When it prompted me to enter a location, I simply typed in the word *Saturn*.

With a whine of electric motors, the telescope automatically swung to find Saturn and focused on the planet.

I leaned into the eyepiece. As always, I nearly gasped at the intensely black sky filled with millions and millions of stars. They were so sharp and clear it seemed I could reach out and grab them.

Hanging in the infinite blackness was Saturn. It wasn't the only planet I'd observed with rings—Jupiter, Uranus, and Neptune also have rings of sorts—but it was definitely the most magnificent.

To you on Earth, it might look like Saturn has only three rings. But from here on Mars, I saw differently. Saturn has thousands of rings, gleaming in reflected sunlight. The rings aren't solid discs but are made of millions of pieces of "dirty ice," ranging in size from a grain of sand to an iceberg as big as a spaceship. Gravity holds them together, and they spin around the planet, some at speeds of 50,000 miles per hour, creating a blur that looks solid to our eyes.

I don't know how long I sat there, marveling at those rings and the incredible sight. Long enough that I saw shadows of some of Saturn's moons drift across the face of the planet. Long enough that I began to pray.

You see, it wasn't until I faced death—I wrote about that in my last journal—that I allowed myself to have faith in God. I realized there must be more to being human than having a mind and body. I realized I have a soul, held within my body. Thinking of it that way has helped me deal with being crippled. In believing I have a soul, I was able to believe in God. Of course, as Mom says, that's only the first step of a great journey. She says once you accept that, then each day is learning more about what that means. How God loves you, how you try to love God in return. And how knowing all of this helps you through the good and bad of life.

Looking through the telescope at the marvels of the universe, I now find it easier and easier to believe that God is behind it. That the creation of the universe was carefully planned out by God, and he's still watching over it. Over us. It has given me comfort, too, to know that a lot of scientists look at the universe and say it points us to God.

Rawling is one of those scientists. He says a lot of things show that the universe was designed for the single reason of producing human life. It's something we've talked about a lot in the short time since he became director.

With Saturn there in front of me, so beautiful and awesome and stunning, it just seemed natural to close my eyes briefly and pray to God, thanking him for allowing me to see such beauty. It may sound strange if you don't pray much, but when I finished, I felt peaceful. I felt as if I did belong, I did have a purpose, and I was supposed to be part of God's creation. I felt as if a load had been taken off my shoulders. Since God made me and had a plan, maybe I didn't have to worry so much about things I couldn't control.

This peace lasted only as long as it took for one other person to step onto the third level near the telescope.

"Hello," she said. She did that tilting thing, hand on her hip, as if "hello" were also some kind of challenge. "I've been looking for you."

It was Ashley.

And this time I wouldn't be able to hide behind a robot body.

CHAPTER 12

"You've been looking for me?" I asked.

"Sure," Ashley said. She grinned. It changed her. Without that grin, she looked grown up. With it, she looked like a tomboy. "Everyone else here is ancient. Over 30. I asked if there was anyone close to my age—I'm 13—and people told me about you."

She stuck her hand out, just like earlier when she'd introduced herself to the robot body. "My name's Ashley. Ashley Jordan."

"Tyce," I said, taking her hand and shaking it. "Tyce Sanders." I was glad it was dim up here at the telescope. For some reason, my ears felt like they were burning red.

"Looked like you were sleeping at the telescope," she said, grinning. As if it wasn't a big deal that I was in a wheelchair.

"Not that I was spying or anything, but when I walked up, you didn't hear me."

"I was . . . I was . . ." I only hesitated because, to me, praying was a private thing—and very new. But I decided I wasn't going to lie about it. There was no shame in trying to understand the mystery of life and seeing God behind it. So I took a deep breath and explained. "I was praying. When I look through the telescope, it blows me away. I can't help but think and wonder about God."

"Cool." Ashley flipped back her hair, revealing her silver cross earrings. "I respect someone who's not afraid to ask questions about God. There's so much to figure out. What I've found is that when you think about this universe as being created instead of just happening by accident, you start to see God everywhere in all these amazing things. Wait until you get into Einstein's theory of relativity. Energy turning into matter. Matter turning into energy. Wow! What really messes with my mind is the relationship between time and the speed of light. Think about it. At the speed of light, time slows down to a stop. If you could ride a light beam across the universe, a billion, billion, billion, billion miles later, not one second of time would have passed for you, even though hundreds of years would have passed by on Earth. It makes me think that if God doesn't exist in the same sense we do in our bodies, it's only natural that he would be outside of space and time as we know it."

She laughed at my expression. "You can shut your jaw now. Your mouth is open so wide you could catch flies, if Mars had flies. What? You don't think a girl should know about stuff like that?"

I lifted my hand and pushed my jaw shut. It made her laugh again.

"It's not that you're a girl," I said. "I mean, my mom's a scientist. It's just that I never expected the one person my age in this dome to turn out to be someone who loves science too."

"How could I not?" Ashley answered. "Considering the family I was born into."

"What kind of family?"

She answered my question with a question. "What do you do for fun around here?"

If she didn't want to talk about her family, I wasn't going to push it. "For fun?" I shrugged. "Dance lessons. Try out for Olympic sprinting competitions. Things like that."

"But you're in a . . ." She hit her forehead with the heel of her palm. "Sorry. You were joking, weren't you?"

Another shrug. "Bad habit," I said.

"Don't get me started on my bad habits. Let me tell you, six months crossing the solar system with no music or friends . . . well, halfway here I nearly asked them to drop me off without a space suit."

"Um," I began, intensely curious but not wanting to pry, "exactly what are you doing here?"

"My father is a quantum physicist. That's why I know so much about relativity and stuff like that. He's setting up some research that's a lot easier here than on Earth because of the lower gravity. He's so good that when he told the United Nations' science agency he wouldn't go unless he could take me, they said it would be all right, since I was the only kid in our family."

Just like me. An only kid. And a science freak. Wow! "What about your mother?"

Ashley stiffened, as rigid as a statue.

Dumb, I told myself. I'd just asked about her family again. "Sorry," I said.

"Don't worry about it," she said quietly, her eyes turned downward. "I'd have asked the same question. They got divorced about a year ago. It was just pretty messy, that's all. I think Dad wanted to be sent out here to get away from her."

"I'm sorry," I said and meant it. I knew what having an absent parent was like.

"Me too," Ashley said sadly. Then she smiled, but it seemed forced. "You want to help me with something?"

"Probably," I said. With every passing minute, it was getting easier to be around her. I felt less shy.

"Help me find this robot," she said. "I met him earlier and—"

"Him?"

"His name was Bruce. He's kind of a smarty-pants, but it's cute."

"Oh, Bruce. You met him already?"

Ashley nodded.

"Smart robot," I said, playing along. "Knows his math."

"I was impressed," she said.

"Wait until you catch his juggling act."

"Bruce the robot can juggle?" Her eyes widened like a little girl hearing about Santa Claus.

"Sure," I replied. "You'll know he really likes you if he offers to show you."

"Cool."

"Why do you want to find him?" I asked.

"He promised me a tour of the dome."

"He spends most of his nights plugged into the electrical grid," I said. I wasn't going to mention that tonight he was lying in the middle of the greenhouse, destroyed by aliens.

"Oh. I know he's just a robot. But that sounds lonely."

"He'll be all right. He . . ." I pictured the robot. Stuck in the middle of the bamboo corn. At the edge of a small gully. A gully made by water from the nozzles of the greenhouse sprinklers. Which meant the robot was directly beneath . . .

"He what?" Ashley asked.

I thought of the last things I'd heard and felt in the robot body. Click. Hiss. Then something cold against the body.

"Got to go," I said and started wheeling quickly away from her toward the ramp. "Good-bye."

"But . . . ," she began to protest.

I didn't hear the rest of it. By then I was already whizzing down the ramp to find Rawling.

CHAPTER 13

I couldn't sleep after talking with Rawling about my theory. I kept thinking about what I'd be doing the next morning. So in the quiet of the night I worked on my journal. I realized even if no one on Earth ever read it, I'd at least have it for myself. Years and years down the road, as an old man, I could reread all this and remember what it was like growing up on Mars.

Keeping that in mind, I pretended I was writing a letter to myself in the future. That made it fun as I finished explaining in my journal what had made me leave Ashley so quickly.

Aliens hadn't stalled the robot body. It was water. At least, that was my theory.

When Ashley asked me about Bruce—a dumb name, but it stuck—and when I thought about the robot beneath the water nozzles, the last sounds and sensations made sense.

Click. That was the automatic timer.

Hiss. That was the beginning of the water spray.

And the cold sensation? Water.

My robot body had been standing at the gully where the water came down and collected. Water, then, had showered my titanium shell.

It was so obvious that after I rushed to find Rawling and tell him my theory, he groaned.

Rawling searched the computer records to find out exactly when I left the robot body and went into the thrashing fit on the bed. That time matched exactly when the automatic sprinklers in the greenhouse began to spray water. Which was not good for Bruce.

On Mars, it never rains. Water is a precious resource. The dome was established near the south, where we can get water from the polar ice cap. Because water is so scarce, no one bothered to wonder what would happen to the robot body if it got wet.

So what would happen to a robot body suddenly soaked in water? An electrical short circuit, if my theory is right.

In the morning, Rawling is going to try to hook me up to the robot body again. Then we'll find out more about the aliens. It will only work, of course, if the robot body is still fine and we can get there before the automatic sprinklers turn on again.

But we won't find out until morning. And if it is fine . . .

"Tyce?" It was my father's voice. He knocked on the door. "Yes," I called.

He pushed open the door. It was dim inside my room, with only the computer monitor giving light. "Up late, aren't you?" He was framed in the doorway with light behind him, so I couldn't see his expression.

"I'm not a kid," I said quickly. "Mom doesn't tell me when to go to bed anymore."

"Hang on," my father said. "You don't need to get so defensive. I didn't say there was anything wrong with it. It was just a comment."

"In that case," I said, "you're right. I am up late."

"I don't appreciate your tone of voice."

Well, I thought, I don't appreciate someone who shows up every three years and tells me what to do. But I didn't say it. I saved my file and clicked off my computer instead. When the monitor light dimmed, only the light from the common living area lit the room.

"Good night," I said. "I'm tired."

"Good night? But you were just—"

"I finished my computer work. I've got to get up early tomorrow," I stated flatly as I wheeled to my bed.

"Tyce, I don't understand why you act like this. I'm only trying to talk with you—"

I cut my father's words off. "Really, I'm very tired."

I heard him expel a breath. Then he left the room and shut the door without another word.

It left me in complete darkness.

For some stupid reason, I felt like crying.

CHAPTER 14

"Yesterday when you were out, I ran diagnostics through the remote and couldn't get a reading," Rawling said. His hair had rooster points, sticking up as if he hadn't had time to comb it yet. "But this morning everything checked out fine. If your theory about water is right, that would explain it."

We were back in the computer lab. I'd escaped the minidome without a lecture from Mom about how my father was doing his best and that he and I should try to get along.

I nodded in agreement with Rawling. "Whatever water leaked inside would have dried up after you ran the first diagnostics."

He checked his watch. "The next automatic watering takes place in just under an hour. I want the robot out of the greenhouse before then. Even if you're not directly beneath a nozzle this time, you'll still get some of the spray."

Rawling lifted my legs onto the bed for me. He began to strap me down. "Everything checks out fine with the robot. Still, I wish we could bring it in for a visual inspection. Any other circumstances but this . . ."

Again, I nodded. I felt sorry for Rawling. As new director, this alien issue must be stressful. He was hours away from the deadline he'd set for himself to tell everybody under the dome about the aliens. If all he could tell them was what little we knew, it would raise the level of fear so high that his announcement could do more harm than good. We definitely needed to find out more about those aliens.

"Rawling?"

"Yes?"

"I've got to ask. I've been trying to figure it out myself, and I can't get anywhere with it."

"Ask."

"What if there are aliens? So far, we don't have any proof, except for what I might have seen, but that could be a water short circuit messing up the robot computer, or maybe me trying to imagine too hard I was seeing something. But what if there are aliens? Then how does God fit into this?"

"Why don't you ask me the square root of 5,237,676?" Rawling fired back.

"Huh?"

He smiled. "Well, that wouldn't be much tougher of a question than your first one." He thought for a moment. "I'm not sure I can give you a good answer, Tyce. On one hand, it's God's universe, and who are we to say what he can or cannot do in it? On the other hand, as humans, we naturally want to feel he loves only us in a special way. You have a special relationship with your mom, but does that mean that she's allowed to love only you?"

Ouch. So Rawling had noticed how I felt about my father. At least Rawling was being honest with me.

"Does that help?" he asked.

"No." I grinned.

Rawling grinned too. "Never be afraid to ask questions about God. Even if it doesn't look like you'll get the answers right away. God is big enough to handle anything you might ask."

"Sure," I said. "Thanks."

"Ready for the blindfold?"

"Ready."

"Remember," he said as he put the blindfold over my head. "If anything feels or looks strange once you get in there, give the stop command and return here. Got it?"

"Got it," I said.

Rawling ran through our checklist.

When we'd reviewed everything to his satisfaction, he put the soundproof headset over my ears.

In the darkness and silence of waiting, I was nervous. If my theory was wrong . . .

I told myself that fear wasn't going to help me. As that thought ended, once again I began to fall off a high, invisible cliff into a deep, invisible hole. I kept falling and falling and falling. . . .

CHAPTER 15

I stopped falling and opened my eyes among the stalks of bamboo corn in the greenhouse. Light filtered into my front video lens. Mentally, I blinked. The robot had no need to blink the way I did in my human body, but it felt natural and brought the green of the bamboo corn into focus.

I turned the video lens upward and brought the ceiling of the greenhouse into focus. I'd been right. Directly above me was a sprinkler nozzle. It would have completely flooded my robot body with water.

As Rawling had instructed me, I began a checklist of the other robot senses.

Sight, of course, was operational.

I went to hearing next. Without moving, I strained for any unusual sounds.

What reached me was the distant sigh of wind moving
through small rips in the plastic fabric of the greenhouse
tent. No scurrying of alien creatures. And something else.
Something strange.

I turned up my hearing volume.

There it was. A slow and steady and very soft thump-
thump-thump-thump. Like a heartbeat? Or heartbeats?

Sight and sound worked fine. Maybe too fine. The
heartbeats made me feel like I was in some kind of horror
movie.

"Hello?" I said. My voice worked fine too.

My robot body couldn't smell or taste. So I let my mind
go to the last of the senses. Touch. I became aware of another
sensation through my robot body. Weight. And warmth. In my
right hand.

The robot was so strong that I hadn't noticed the weight
at first. To my senses, it felt like a watch on a human's wrist.
Almost no weight at all. But there was definitely weight and
warmth hitting the sensors embedded in the titanium of my
three fingers.

I slowly turned my front video lens downward. At the
same time, I lifted my right hand.

At first all I saw was a blurry darkness. From looking
upward at the ceiling, my focus had been set on a distance
farther away. Like an automatic camera, the lens zoomed in
to make an adjustment.

When I saw what I was holding, I finally realized where the thump-thump-thump came from.

It *was* a heartbeat—from the small Martian creature gripped securely in my titanium fingers.

CHAPTER 16

I shouted *Stop!* in my mind.

Instantly I was back in my body. My human body. On the bed in the computer lab. "Rawling," I said as calmly as I could.

I didn't hear his reply, though, not with the soundproof headset over my ears.

Seconds later, he took off my blindfold and removed the headset. "You all right?" He looked worried. He quickly began to unstrap me from the bed.

"I'm all right," I answered. "Don't unstrap me. I want to go back. I just needed to ask you something. Not via robot but person to person." It felt strange, staring straight up at the ceiling while I talked.

"Ask away."

"Well," I said. This was going to be fun. Which is why I wanted to ask my question in person. "What do you want me to do with the alien I captured?"

"What!" Rawling shouted in my ear.

"Alien," I repeated. "I've got it in my hand. My robot hand. You want me to let it go? Or bring it into the dome?"

"Alien! What's it look like? How'd you capture it so quickly? Is it alive? dead? Talk to me!" he said excitedly.

I was right. This was fun. "Remember I told you all these dark objects were jumping toward me as I blacked out in the greenhouse?"

Rawling nodded.

"I brought my hands up to protect myself," I said. "One of them must have jumped into my hand. As the robot lost power, the fingers locked into place. The poor thing must have been stuck in the robot hand for nearly 24 hours."

"Poor thing?"

"It's almost cute." I stopped myself. "Correction: it is cute." I tried to think of a way to explain it. I had to rely on photos I'd seen in the digital encyclopedia. "It looks like a mixture between a koala bear and a small puppy. It has thick dark hair, a mixture of brown and black. Not much for a nose. Big paws. Big eyes, two of them. Four legs. Two ears that hang down. A mouth."

"But small enough to fit in your hand."

"Not really," I said. I had seen photos of people holding

cats and dogs, so I had an idea of the size of those animals. "Bigger than a cat. I caught it under the front legs. Most of the body is hanging out of my hand."

"Alive?"

"Yes. But not really doing much. I think it's close to dead."

"Unbelievable," Rawling said. He drew a sharp breath, then let it out with a whistle.

"Believe it. That's why I'm back. I didn't know if you wanted me to bring it to the dome or not. I didn't want to do anything until I'd talked to you about it."

"Yes, bring it back," he said. A second later, he shook his head. "No. It might die in dome air if it's not used to breathing oxygen."

Rawling began to pace the room. "What if it's carrying alien viruses or alien bacteria? If we bring it into the dome, who knows what damage those viruses could do to human bodies? Especially human bodies in a closed space like this."

He paced more. "But if it's close to dying, we need to try to save it. Do you have any idea what it would mean to science to be able to examine a living alien life-form?"

"How about if you drive a platform buggy out to the cornfield?" I asked. "Wear a space suit, and let all the oxygen out of the platform dome. I'll bring the alien out to you, and you can examine it in the platform buggy."

Rawling stopped pacing. "Brilliant. Very brilliant. I'll

take Jim Harrington with me. He's the best geneticist we have."

With Rawling's praise, I felt proud—like he was my father. It was too bad my father and I couldn't talk like this.

"One other thing before you put me back in the robot body," I told Rawling.

"What's that?"

"When you leave the dome in the platform buggy, make sure you take some water for our little friend."

"Water?"

"Yes. Where I was standing was right below a sprinkler. I don't think those creatures were attacking me. I think they wanted water. When they heard the clicking of the automatic timer, they knew the sprinklers were about to start. I think they wanted to get at the water in that little gully before it evaporated."

CHAPTER 17

I opened my eyes again in the robot body. The little koala-bear alien was still in my right hand.

I rolled away from the gully and began wheeling toward the entrance of the greenhouse.

I stopped. Had I heard correctly? I turned up my hearing.

Yes. It was a mewing sound, coming from the little alien in my hand. I lifted it and looked directly into its large brown eyes. With its last energy, it was trying to call out.

I heard another mewing sound answer from somewhere in the bamboo corn nearby.

My visual only showed thick green leaves, so I switched to infrared.

There it was! A glowing red shape, maybe 10 feet away,

the size of the alien in my hand. It was calling to the alien I was taking away.

I switched back to visual. The alien's large dark eyes made me feel sorry for it. I reminded myself that these creatures had attacked Timothy Neilson and ripped his space suit to shreds.

It mewed again.

"Sorry, little guy," I said in a soft voice. "I do not have much choice. We will get you some water, and maybe you will feel better."

Was it my imagination, or did it perk up at the sound of my voice?

I began to wheel toward the entrance again. The mewing followed me to the edge of the bamboo corn.

At the entrance, I switched to the rear lens and looked for the other alien. It stayed hidden as I left the greenhouse, but the mewing grew louder, as if the creature was saying good-bye to the alien I'd captured.

Great, I thought. Now I am a galactic bully.

I turned my focus ahead, toward the dome. The sky had turned from early-morning butterscotch to a reddish pink. The sun was a dark blue. The wind had dropped, and the temperature had risen. It was a great day to be outside on Mars in a robot body. A great day, that is, for sightseeing.

But I had other duties.

In the empty space of sand between the dome and the

greenhouse, I saw the platform buggy on its giant wheels racing toward me and headed forward to meet it. As it got closer, I saw two men in space suits. I couldn't see their faces behind the dark visors, but I guessed it was Rawling McTigre and Jim Harrington. Dust sprayed me and the little alien as the monstrous vehicle lurched to a stop in front of us.

One of the space-suited men stepped out of the small, clear dome on top of the platform. He carried a Plexiglas cage in one hand and held the railing with the other as he climbed down the ladder. When he dropped lightly on the ground, he opened the cage without saying a single word of greeting. His visor was as dark as sunglasses, and I couldn't see his face.

"Rawling?" I queried.

Still silent, the man extended the cage toward me.

"Dr. Harrington?"

No reply. The man in the space suit just pointed at the empty cage.

I obeyed his unspoken command and gently put the alien inside.

The man turned around and began climbing up the ladder.

"Is Rawling with you?" I shouted. "Can you tell me what is happening?"

The man ignored me and continued his ascent. Seconds later he entered the platform buggy's dome. And seconds after that, the platform buggy jerked forward, turned, and sped back toward the dome.

Strange. Very strange.

It seemed like I was no longer part of this. Even if it did look as if I'd discovered the first alien life-form known to humankind.

CHAPTER 18

When I woke up on the bed in the computer lab, I was alone.

At least I thought I was alone. Because I was blindfolded and wearing the soundproof headset, I had no way of knowing if anyone else was in the room. And because I was strapped to the bed, I couldn't move my hands to lift the blindfold.

"Hello?" I called out into the dark silence. "Rawling? Anyone?" I waited.

Nothing.

Five minutes later, still nothing. I was glad I didn't have to go to the bathroom.

Another five minutes, still nothing.

I shouted, "Rawling! Anyone!"

This was not fun. I had parked the robot body in a dry

part of the greenhouse and given the stop command to return to my body on this bed. Now I felt like a prisoner.

"Rawling! Anyone!"

When the touch to my shoulder came, I nearly had a heart attack. The straps were undone first. That should have been my first clue. Rawling always took off the soundproof headset first, then the blindfold.

As soon as my arms were free, I lifted my hands and pulled off my blindfold. Then my headset. "Oh," I said. "Hi."

"I was looking for you," my father said. "And from what your mom's told me about your recent virtual-reality simulations with the robot, I figured you might be at the lab. I'd just reached the door when I heard you call out."

"Thanks," I said.

"You all right?" He looked tired and worried. I could tell he hadn't shaved yet, and his hair was messy. Because of all the love on his face, I wanted to tell him I was sorry for being such a jerk the night before.

But I just couldn't do it. So I simply said, "Yes, I'm all right."

"I thought you were always supposed to be under supervision," my father said. "Where's Rawling?"

"Right here." While my father and I were talking, Rawling had stepped into the room.

My father faced Rawling. "This is unusual. I thought he was supposed to be under supervision."

"Yes," Rawling snapped. "Believe me. This is unusual."

I struggled to sit up on the bed. "What's happening?" I asked angrily. "Out there you don't say a word when you arrive with the platform buggy. I wake up here and I'm all alone. It's like once you had the—"

Rawling cut off my words. "Could Tyce and I speak in private?" he asked my father.

"Not until you tell me what's going on," my father replied firmly.

"Look, I'm sorry," Rawling said. "I'll explain soon. But for security reasons, I need to speak with your son in private."

My father didn't reply to Rawling. Instead he said to me, "Are you all right with that?"

I was glad he allowed me to speak for myself. I nodded.

"I'll go," my father told Rawling, "but I've already seen enough to make me wonder what's going on. Let me tell you this. Mess with Tyce, and you mess with me. Got it? As Tyce's dad, I won't fight his battles for him, but I'll fight his battles with him."

I was surprised at his tone. And suddenly proud. I almost asked him to stay.

But he marched out too fast, the anger showing in his quick steps and the straightness of his shoulders.

"You left me alone out there," I said to Rawling. "Then alone in here. And what about the alien?"

"There was no alien," he said.

"Sure there was," I argued. "I saw you take it into the dome. It was—"

"There was no alien," Rawling said. "It's that simple. No alien. Now I suggest you go back to your minidome."

"But—"

"No alien. I refuse to talk about this subject with you anymore." Despite his stern words, Rawling seemed to be quietly pleading with me.

Confused by his sudden change in attitude, I wondered what was making him act this way. It had to be something beyond his control. Still, it made me mad. "Come on. You can't—"

"I can do anything I want. I'm the director of the Mars Project, and I have almost unlimited authority. Please don't make me call security to escort you to your minidome." With that, Rawling turned and left too.

CHAPTER 19

"Hello, Mr. Neilson," I said kindly to the man on the hospital bed. "Glad to see you're doing better."

If his condition hadn't been so serious—he'd been in a coma—I might have wanted to laugh at how he looked. He was completely bald, and his face sagged with wrinkles so he resembled a round-headed basset hound. His eyes were black and blue from where he had slammed against his space-suit visor.

"I'm glad to be doing better," he answered.

I nodded. "I have to tell you, when I picked you up in the greenhouse, it looked pretty bad." I was probably fishing for a compliment, expecting he might thank me for saving his life, because he'd said so little since I wheeled into the hospital room to visit him.

"I don't know what you're talking about," Neilson replied.

Then I realized he'd hit his head hard enough to knock himself out. The space suit had lost air and heat. No wonder he couldn't remember. So I tried to fill him in. "No one told you? You were in the greenhouse. Something was chasing you. You fell down. Your space suit was ripped. They sent a robot in to get you."

"It's not good to make up stories," he said, frowning at me.

"I'm not," I insisted.

"I was collecting rock samples," Neilson explained. "I fell and tumbled for quite a distance. Jagged rocks ripped my space suit. Meds in a platform buggy rescued me."

Why was he lying? Nobody collected rock samples in the greenhouse. "I was there," I said. "I saw different."

"You were there? A kid in a wheelchair?"

"I mean I was there, controlling a robot body. I saw the path in the greenhouse where you'd been running."

"Not true."

"But I can prove it. There was a voice recording. You said something was chasing you. I heard it. That's why I'm here. To ask you about that."

"You're mistaken. Stop bothering me with this nonsense. I need to rest."

"Nonsense? It's not nonsense. It's—"

"Med! Med!" Timothy Neilson called loudly to another

room. "Could you ask this young man to leave? He persists in bothering me."

Seconds later, a large man appeared with Rawling behind him.

"Tyce," Rawling said sternly, "this man needs recovery time. He took a bad spill down a cliff. Maybe you should go now."

"Down a cliff! Come on. He was in—"

"Enough," Rawling warned me. "Say good-bye."

I could tell it was useless to argue.

"Furthermore," Rawling continued, "I suggest you talk about this with no one else. Including your parents."

"Or else?" I said angrily, not believing this was the Rawling I'd known for years. What had gotten into him?

"Or else they will be shipped back to Earth," he said bluntly.

I turned my wheelchair and pushed past him. I was getting kicked out. Just like a half hour earlier, I'd been kicked out of Dr. Harrington's office when I'd gone to ask him how the alien was doing.

Now I was really, really mad.

CHAPTER 20

I was beginning to find that writing in my journal helped me get my thoughts straight. Early in the evening, instead of going to the telescope as I often did, I stayed in our minidome and began to type on the keyboard.

I wrote all the things I knew for sure about what had happened.

Earlier in the day I captured an alien. Two men in space suits met me in a platform buggy and took the alien into the dome. Since then Rawling has pretended the alien doesn't exist. Dr. Harrington refuses to talk to me. Timothy Neilson acts like he wasn't attacked by these aliens.

I was in the middle of a big stretch and yawn when I thought of something else. I banged away at my keyboard.

Something is strange. Rawling told me he didn't want the alien inside the dome because our air might kill it and because it might have alien viruses or alien bacteria that might hurt humans. But the men in the space suits immediately took the alien into the dome. Does that mean they already knew it was safe for the alien and for us? If it is safe, could that mean it isn't truly an alien?

That's as far as I got with my journal. I knew who could help me with this question.

"Mom!" I shouted. "Mom!" I pushed away from the computer and rolled toward my door. "Mom! Mom!"

She met me at the doorway.

"I have to ask you something."

"That's it? Yelling like that and all you have is a question?"

"A big question. About genetic experiments."

Mom moved to my bed and sat on the edge.

I wheeled around to face her. "How does it work? When you try to make a different kind of plant? You know, the DNA and stuff like that."

"How long an answer do you want?"

"Short. Like an overview."

She nodded. "Picture a circle with a dot in the center."

"Done."

"That's a simple drawing of a cell under a microscope. The circle is the outer wall. Everything inside the circle and around the dot is plasma with nutrients. The dot in the center is the nucleus. The nucleus is the computer software that runs the cell. Got it?"

"Got it."

"As a biologist, I can only marvel at how the nucleus is so simple yet so complex. It contains the DNA you mentioned, which is microscopic strands of protein. This protein is in the form of a double helix, which is the shape of a ladder that has been twisted into a spiral. Still with me?"

"Still with you."

"The double helix shape lets the DNA duplicate perfectly, so that one cell can photocopy itself a trillion times and it will still be a perfect copy, no mistakes. That's important to genetic experiments. Very important."

"Important," I said.

"Let's talk about flies, for example. Every creature, including a human, begins as one cell. That cell divides and divides and divides. As it divides, the DNA of the cells programs the different cells to specialize. Some cells become skin cells, other cells become eye cells, and so on."

"I'm listening."

"What's absolutely mind-boggling," Mom said, showing her excitement for her work, "is that the DNA packed into that single first cell contains the entire genetic code for that creature or plant. One cell, hundreds of times smaller than the head of a pin, contains the blueprint to build a fly. Or a sheep. Or a monkey. DNA is incredible. That's partly why I first began to believe in God—because it was too difficult to believe that something this amazing could develop by accident."

I nodded. "Experiments . . ."

"Yes. Experiments. Decades ago, back in the 20th century, scientists realized it would be very simple to change a species. All they had to do was change the DNA when it was at the one-cell stage. Let me put it this way. Is it easier to change a trillion cells, or is it easier to change the original cell and let the changes in that first cell be programmed into every cell as it divides?"

"No-brainer," I said. "Get to the first cell."

"That's what they did. I remember reading about one of the first genetic experiments on fruit flies. Scientists changed the DNA that programmed eye growth. When these flies hatched, they had up to 14 pairs of eyes. Eyes on their legs, wings, backs, chest. Scientists had created mutant flies."

"Wow."

"Then in the 1990s scientists learned how to clone animals, and suddenly genetics became scary. It was possible to literally create new species."

"Could they do this to humans?"

Mom rubbed her face. "Yes. Even before the year 2000, the technology to do this was possible. And then the worst happened. An unethical scientist not only cloned humans but also experimented on them to make them taller and stronger. They nicknamed him the new Dr. Frankenstein. He made a mistake, however, and his clones were born without arms. That was AD 2020. It made such an uproar that the government finally stepped in. Very strict laws were created and enforced."

"But," I said, "it is possible to try to create new species."

"It's possible. For the last 30 years, continuing public outrage has made it difficult for scientists on Earth to get funding for any genetic experiments of that type." She smiled. "Plant experiments are one thing, but on animals, no way. Just like smoking in public places or drinking and driving, it has become unthinkable."

"On Earth," I said thoughtfully. "Unthinkable on Earth."

Mom snorted. "Unthinkable anywhere in the solar system. If anyone tried it on Mars and the public on Earth found out, it would threaten the billions of dollars of government support needed to keep this project going forward."

"Thanks," I told her.

"Why are you asking all of this?"

"Curiosity," I answered. "And you've been a big help."

She had been. Genetic experiments to create an animal that would survive on Mars would be top secret.

Now I had to find a way to prove that those experiments existed.

CHAPTER 21

"Greetings, earthling." I found Ashley in the same spot I always went when I wanted to be alone. Up at the telescope.

She jumped. "Bruce!"

"Yes. You remember me, then."

I was in the robot body, of course. Back in the computer lab, in my wired jumpsuit, I had set up the software by myself. My own body was in the wheelchair, with the blindfold and headset I'd put on myself. The only risk I was taking was that I might move in the wheelchair and break the connection. If that happened, I convinced myself it would not damage my body. I hoped. And I also hoped that Rawling wouldn't stop by the lab during the time I was hooked up to the robot's body.

"Remember you? Certainly. You promised me a tour of the dome."

"You will have your tour," I continued in my cheesy robot voice. "However, I wish for you to help me first."

"Sure. It's not like I have anything else to do." Ashley put her hand on my robot shoulder. "That kid Tyce was talking about you. Do you know him?"

"Yes. A very fine human specimen. Smart. Handsome. Witty. You would do well to spend much time with him."

"Huh. Last time we talked, he ran away."

"It must have been important business," I said. "Perhaps later tonight you will see him."

"Well," she said, smiling, "there is a reason I was waiting up here. Not many guys I know can talk science like he does."

"Perhaps you find him to be, as you humans say, appealing in a handsome way?"

"What kind of robot are you?"

I decided to change the subject. "One in need of help. Please."

"Back to that again. What would you like me to do?"

I explained in my finest nasal robot voice.

She agreed.

CHAPTER 22

Five minutes later, I was on the Martian landscape.

I had needed Ashley to help me leave the dome. Alongside the large doors that allowed platform buggies to come in and out, there was a set of small doors to give entrance or exit for men and women in space suits. Ashley had punched in the number sequence on the control pad and promised to wait to let me in when I returned.

I did not expect it to take long. I needed five minutes to get to the greenhouse, five minutes to return, and however long it would take me inside to accomplish my mission.

My wheels whirred along the hard-packed sand. The sky was dark. A ghostly white object whizzed overhead. Phobos—one of the Martian moons. I knew if I waited outside, soon I would see Deimos, the other moon, whizzing in the opposite direction.

But I wasn't going to wait.

I had a small cage in one hand and a container of water in the other. I was gambling that I knew why the alien creatures stayed in the greenhouse. I believed they needed the oxygen given off by the plants to survive as well as the water that came down from the automatic sprinklers.

If I was right about a few things, it wouldn't take me long to capture another one.

And I was right, at least about one thing. There were more of them inside. Or at least one.

Within a minute of going inside, among the darkness of the plants, my infrared spotted a tiny red glow. It was exactly where I'd left behind the second alien earlier. As if it was waiting for its friend to return.

Would I be right about my second guess?

Since the robot body gave off no heat and no human smell, I hoped the creatures wouldn't be afraid of it.

As for my third guess, I'd find out as soon as I opened the water container.

I put the cage down, opened the water container, and set it inside the cage. I did not back away from the cage. If my second and third guesses were right . . .

My infrared showed the second alien moving closer, at first slowly, then quickly. Had it smelled the water?

Yes!

It came out of the darkness of the bamboo corn and into the open.

Would it be afraid of the presence of my robot body?

No!

It moved almost to the cage, so close that I could have bent down and grabbed it.

I didn't, of course. I wanted it in the cage.

Ten seconds later, it stepped inside and began to lap at the water.

I saw the red glows of other creatures approaching, drawn by the water they must have sensed as it evaporated quickly in the dry atmosphere.

All I needed, however, was one. This one. The friend to the one I had captured earlier. I snapped the cage shut before the creature could move away from the water.

I had it! The first step of my plan had gone off without a hitch.

Unfortunately, that was only the beginning of what I needed to do during the rest of the evening.

CHAPTER 23

"Perhaps, earthling, we shall tour the dome later." I was back inside, with my robot body carrying the cage.

But Ashley wasn't listening to Bruce. Her attention was on the cage. "What is that?" she asked, pointing.

"A lost, lonely Martian animal," I said.

"An alien!"

"A lost, lonely Martian animal. Are you deaf?"

Ashley shook her head in evident disgust at the robot and the robot voice. "Whoever it was who made you smart enough to talk to people should have done something about that voice."

"Earthling is not funny," I said.

She was ignoring me again, trying to look in the cage. Fortunately, it was midevening, and most of the scientists and techies were in their minidomes. I had counted on that.

"Please take this to the kid named Tyce," I said. "You will find him at the ramp that leads up to the second level." I handed her the cage. "Earthling, do not open it," I said.

"I'm tired of this 'earthling' stuff. My name is Ashley."

It was my turn to ignore her. I spun around and wheeled away.

"Hey!" she said. "Come back here!"

Too late. I was gone.

I opened my eyes in the wheelchair in the computer lab.

I had parked Bruce the robot at his power charger. Later tonight, I'd plug him in. But now I had to make it to the bottom of the ramp as quickly as possible.

I gripped the wheels of my chair and shoved forward. My legs might be useless, but any of the scientists or techies who arm-wrestled me always lost. I worked my arms hard as I raced to meet Ashley at the bottom of the ramp.

I could see her ahead in the dimness of the lights set at evening level. She stood near the ramp, looking in all directions. The cage was at her feet.

Seconds later, I pulled up. "Hello," I said.

"Oh, hello, Mr. Rude," Ashley said sarcastically, her hands on her hips. "Going to take off on me again without any warning? Between you and that dumb robot, it's enough to—"

She stopped as she noticed what I was doing. "Hey! Bruce told me not to open the cage. You can't—"

I'd already done it—opened the cage. The little Martian creature crawled forward. It paused, then scampered away.

"I can't believe you just did that," Ashley said. "Now what are we going to do?"

"Follow," I said calmly. "Think you can keep up with me?"

"Sure, but how are you going to follow it?"

I grinned and pulled a handheld computer unit from my lap. "GPS. We have them on Mars too."

"Great. What are you going to do? Throw it at that thing? It's long gone."

I flicked on the switch. Immediately, it began beeping.

"Come on," I told Ashley. "This should be fun."

CHAPTER 24

It was fun.

While I was in the robot body, crossing the sand from the greenhouse tent back to the dome, I had attached an emergency tracking device onto the back of the little, furry Martian koala. It meant that now I'd be able to track it wherever it went in the dome.

I hoped that if it was able to smell water, it would also be able to smell its partner, the little guy I'd taken away from it.

Beep-beep-beep-beep.

I left the GPS in my lap as I wheeled forward. Ashley stayed close behind. The signal grew louder as we neared the laboratories at the far end of the dome.

"What's this about, anyway?" Ashley asked.

"I'm not 100 percent sure," I said. "But I think it's about

illegal experiments and some people trying to hide those experiments."

I kept pushing as I spoke. I thought about the rod in my spine—and how the operation that had placed it there had left me crippled. "Someday I'll tell you what it's like to be experimented on when you aren't given the chance to decide for yourself." Just as I suspected that someone was experimenting on the Martian koalas.

Beep-beep-beep-beep. The signal grew louder and quicker.

We were almost there. We faced a row of laboratory doors.

Beep-beep-beep-beep.

"Look!" Ashley exclaimed.

I looked where she was pointing. At the far end of the row, the little Martian creature scratched at a door.

I pulled up.

The sign on the door had big bold letters: Authorized Personnel Only.

"Try the door handle," I suggested.

"I'm not authorized."

"Neither is the little guy trying to get in."

"He's got an excuse. He can't read," Ashley fired back.

I liked her. She was quick. "Fine, then," I said. "Neither can I."

She sighed and tried the handle. It was locked.

I leaned forward and knocked on the door.

"Go away," a voice shouted from inside.

I knocked louder.

This time, no voice answered.

"Inside that room," I told Ashley, "are things that aren't supposed to be happening. For all we know, someone is trying to kill or hide all the experimental animals."

"Who can we report this to?" Ashley said, shocked.

"No one," I answered. I felt bitter and sad about Rawling. By now I'd figured that he was involved somehow. "The director of the Mars Project isn't even interested in stopping this."

"Who else knows about it?"

"You and me."

"Do you think," she asked, "if more people knew what was inside, we could stop this?"

"Maybe," I answered. "Should we try to break down the door?"

The little creature at our feet clawed and scratched to get in.

"No. I've got a better idea." Ashley tilted her head back and screamed louder than I knew any person could scream. She screamed as if a madman were chasing her down. She screamed as if she were in a spaceship headed directly for an asteroid. She screamed as if a huge alien had pulled off one of her arms.

I plugged my ears.

She kept screaming.

It worked. All across the dome, lights began to flick on. Within 30 seconds, dozens of people were running toward us.

Ashley finally stopped. And grinned. "Not bad, huh?"

I grinned back. "Not bad at all."

CHAPTER 25

By the time I was ready for sleep, I wasn't ready for sleep.

Sure, the clock said it was late, but I was still too excited from all the things that had happened since Ashley screamed to the world.

I'd already explained everything to my parents. Now they were asleep, and the minidome was quiet.

That left me one thing I could do—write in my journal and explain it to the old man I would someday become. I fired up my computer and began to tell the rest of it.

Ashley's scream brought dozens of people. Many of them wore pajamas because they'd been asleep or were getting ready for bed. The little Martian koala was still trying to get inside the door, and that was all the proof we needed to convince everyone that inside the lab we'd find at least one more.

It turned out there were dozens in plastic boxes that had been their homes. By the time we got the door open, most of them had been crammed into a storage box.

Dr. Jim Harrington, the head scientist on the illegal experiment, had figured he'd been caught and was trying to get rid of the evidence. We'd stopped him just before he was about to load the genetically altered koalas on a platform buggy and drive them miles away from the dome. He'd planned to leave them to die, trapped in the box. Now it's going to be up to the director to decide what to do.

What would the director do? In the morning, I was going to find out because I intended to sit in Rawling's office until he told me everything else.

I shut off my computer and wheeled over to my bed. I pulled myself out of my wheelchair and got under the covers, then reached over to shut off the light.

I lay awake in the darkness, thinking about everything.

But I wasn't alone. Happy mewing sounds came from a basket in the corner of the bedroom. The two little Martian koalas the robot had captured were snuggled against each other.

I wasn't quite sure what to name them yet. I was just happy that they were finally back together.

Five minutes later, they began to snore.

Wonderful.

CHAPTER 26

I found Rawling at his desk. He lifted his head as I rolled in.

"Good morning," he said.

"If you say so."

He nodded. "You have every right to be mad at me."

"Why should I be mad? Just because you suddenly pretend I don't exist? And that the alien I found doesn't exist? I thought that's what friends always did to each other."

Rawling sighed and stood. He took a piece of paper from his desk and walked it over to me. "My letter of resignation as director," he said, handing the paper to me. "Take a look at the date."

I scanned the letter. It was very short and very polite. It was dated yesterday. "So?" I asked.

"I wrote it and signed it yesterday afternoon. Before

you found the experimental lab. Not after. You probably don't trust me anymore—and I don't blame you—so I can bring up the computer file and show you the last time I worked on the letter to prove I'm not lying."

I gave him back the letter.

"Tyce," he said, his voice softening, "it's important to me that you know I resigned because of what was happening. I was on my way over to explain to you last night when all that screaming brought us to the lab."

Rawling returned to his desk, sat down, and faced me. "Here it is in a nutshell. Yes, unethical secret experiments had been performed with the blessing of the previous direc-tor, Blaine Steven. Dr. Harrington's goal was to take an Earth species and genetically alter it to survive on Mars. He picked koalas because they survive on vegetation and have a relatively low consumption of energy. His ultimate goal was to create a creature that needs low oxygen, builds a thick layer of fat and fur to protect it against cold, and will eat the bamboo corn that will be planted around the planet."

"Why?" I asked.

"Dr. Harrington claims the koalas are intended to be a future food source. But I'm not sure I believe him."

"Because . . . ," I said slowly as I processed this information.

"I'll get to that in a minute. It's one of the reasons I

resigned. But I want to explain what they were doing out in the cornfield."

I nodded. Rawling looked weary. I didn't know whether to feel sorry for him or stay angry.

"Remember the oxygen crisis in the dome? Remember how ex-Director Steven arranged for oxygen tanks to be stolen?"

I nodded again.

"You might not have noticed," Rawling said, "but 20 tanks were stolen, and later only 18 were recovered. I finally found out where the missing two tanks went. To the secret experimental lab. Steven had approved it to keep as many of the experimental animals alive as possible."

"Instead of trying to keep scientists or techies alive?"

"Steven and Harrington thought people were going to die anyway. So why not at least keep these important experiments alive?"

I shook my head in disgust.

"At that time," he continued, "Dr. Harrington realized he didn't have enough oxygen for all his animals to survive. So he released most of them onto the surface of the planet, expecting them to die. He didn't realize how close this new generation was to being able to survive outside the dome. The creatures survived long enough to make it to the greenhouse tent, which evidently had just enough traces of oxygen and water to keep them alive."

I was beginning to understand. "Which Harrington did not know until Timothy Neilson was attacked in the cornfield."

"Not exactly attacked," Rawling said. "These animals are vegetarians. But they were desperate for water. You know no space suit is completely sealed down to a microscopic level. These creatures could smell the trace amounts of moisture that leaked from Neilson's suit. They swarmed him, and he panicked at the sight of what he thought were aliens. When he fell, they ripped holes in his suit looking for the water."

"When I captured one of the koalas, Dr. Harrington realized they could survive outside the dome."

"Yes," he said. "Remember, I said I would get him to help us. Only instead of helping, he took over the operation. I didn't have much choice. Not when he patched me by radio phone to a high government source on Earth who forced me to cooperate in trying to hide the existence of these things. When Neilson woke up from his coma, he was also threatened and forced to lie. From that point on, I was effectively out of it. Nothing to say. Nothing to do."

"That's why you wrote the letter of resignation."

"Yes. And no."

I squinted, puzzled.

"I couldn't believe these experiments were simply to create a future food source. Think about it. Once the scientists learned to genetically alter animals to live on the surface of

Mars, do you think they'd leave it at that? Or would they try to alter humans next? That's where all this genetic stuff gets scary. Knowledge itself is not good or evil. It's what people choose to do with it. Between Steven and Harrington and the high government source on Earth, you've already seen what can happen. I have no doubt that future genetic technology would be used on humans. But not on adult humans who have a choice."

I let out a deep breath. "On human embryos, right? Because that's where the DNA changes have to be made."

"Exactly. My decision yesterday was to take all of this public. But only if you decided I should. That's why I was looking for you when the screaming started."

"Me? Why should it be up to me?" I asked, stunned by the responsibility he was giving me. After all, I was just a kid.

Rawling got up again. Walked around the room. Sat down. "I know you hate being in a wheelchair. I know how much it means to you to have the freedom of that robot body. You're the first human in history to be given that kind of opportunity."

His lips tightened in anger. "As director, I had the power to stop the experimentation. I had the power to bring it to light. And I definitely should have done what was right instead of trying to cover it up and hide it from you."

"What does this have to do with the fact that it was going to be my decision?"

"I was being blackmailed. I was told that if I didn't find a way to keep these experiments secret, you'd be sent back to Earth when the shuttle left in a few months. Away from your family. Away from all you are about to learn on Mars. Away from the freedom of that robot body."

"You were covering this up to protect me." The words came slowly out of my mouth.

"I thought I was. Until I realized something. You of all people know what it's like to be experimented on without permission. And here I was, making another decision about you and your future without your knowledge. That was as wrong as covering up what I knew about the experiment." Rawling looked me square in the eyes. "I hope you can forgive me."

"Sure," I said. "We're friends."

Even as I spoke, I was haunted by guilt. I don't know what I would have decided. Keep my freedom and allow the illegal experiments to continue? Or give up that precious freedom and do what was right—make the experiments public knowledge? I was just glad the decision had been taken from me by Ashley's great screaming job in front of the secret lab.

CHAPTER 27

Half an hour later, I was back in our minidome. Mom had already left for her lab. That left me, my father, and the two little Martian koalas. They were asleep in a basket in the corner. As usual. Koalas on Earth sleep 22 hours a day, and one of the reasons that species had been picked for experiments on Mars was the low amount of energy they burned.

I had things to do too, like telling Ashley what I'd found out from Rawling. But I needed to speak to my father first.

On my way past the sleeping koalas, I stopped and smiled. Their eyes were shut, and they made tiny snoring noises.

I had that smile on my face when I stopped in front of my father. He was drinking coffee and reviewing some technical notes when I cleared my throat. "Dad?" That word came out of my mouth as a surprise. I was so used to thinking of him as "my father," like some uncaring person who bossed me around whenever he showed up.

But I hadn't been able to stop thinking about what he'd said to Rawling in the lab. "Let me tell you this. Mess with Tyce, and you mess with me. Got it? As Tyce's dad, I won't fight his battles for him, but I'll fight his battles with him."

"Dad?" I said again. It felt less strange.

He still held his coffee, but his eyes were on my face, not on the technical notes.

"Yesterday," I began, "I was really hurt about something. Rawling suddenly decided not to talk to me, and I couldn't figure out why. It was like we suddenly weren't friends anymore. Only I had no choice about it."

"I'm sorry to hear that," Dad said.

"It's all right now," I explained. "We had a chance to talk about it."

"Good."

"Yes. And no."

Dad gave me a strange look. Probably the same strange look I'd given Rawling when he'd used those same words a half hour earlier.

"Good because I found out he had a reason for what he did. Bad because it hit me that I'd been doing the same thing to someone else. You."

He set his coffee down.

"You see," I said, "it's not fair for me to do my best to ignore you because I'm mad about stuff. If you have no idea why I'm mad, you probably feel the way I did when Rawling treated me as if I didn't exist."

Dad smiled, but he looked sad. "Now that you mention it . . ."

"Anyway," I said, "I'm sorry."

"Me too," he said. "Do you want to talk about what's bothering you?"

"How much time you got?"

"As much as you need," Dad said. "Let's talk."

CHAPTER 28

Dad and I did talk. Lots.

Over the next month, we became friends again.

Of course, other things happened too. Rawling tried to resign, but his resignation wasn't accepted. The surviving koalas were allowed to live. Harrington and the ex-director were both scheduled to be sent back to Earth when the next shuttle headed back.

And, oh yeah, Ashley and I spent a lot of time hanging out together.

In fact, things were just settling back to normal—as normal as anything might be for humans living under the dome on Mars—when an earthquake hit.

Well, not an earthquake. This was Mars. I guess you'd have to call it a marsquake.

Whatever it was, it was scary. Although it happened at least 200 miles away, it still rocked the dome.

What was even scarier was the fact that it might not have been an accident.

But all this is going to fill another journal. . . .

SCIENCE AND GOD

You've probably noticed that the question of God's existence comes up in Robot Wars.

It's no accident, of course. I think this is one of the most important questions that we need to decide for ourselves. If God created the universe and there is more to life than what we can see, hear, taste, smell, or touch, that means we have to think of our own lives as more than just the time we spend on Earth.

On the other hand, if this universe was not created and God does not exist, then that might really change how you view your existence and how you live.

Sometimes science is presented in such a way that it suggests there is no God. To make any decision, it helps to know as much about the situation as possible. As you decide for yourself, I'd like to show in the Robot Wars series that many, many people—including famous scientists—don't see science this way.

As you might guess, I've spent a lot of time wondering about science and God, and I've spent a lot of time reading about what scientists have learned and concluded. Because of this, I wrote a nonfiction book called *Who Made The Moon?* and you can find information about it at www.whomade-themoon.com. If you ever read it, you'll see why science does not need to keep anyone away from God.

With that in mind, I've added a little bit more to this book—a couple of essays about the science in journals one and two of Robot Wars, based on what you can find in *Who Made The Moon?*

Sigmund Brouwer
whomadethemoon.com

JOURNAL ONE
DOES GOD REALLY EXIST?

Q: *Why do science and faith seem so far apart?*

A: Much of this happened because of how the church in Rome treated a scientist named Galileo in the early 1700s. Galileo supported a new theory that the earth revolved around the sun. But the church insisted the Bible said otherwise. So the pope punished Galileo—he even threatened to have Galileo killed unless he began to teach again that the sun revolved around the earth. After that, many "religious" people thought scientists wanted to attack religion, and scientists became antireligion.

But Galileo, who deeply believed in God, became known as one of the greatest scientists of all time. He predicted that a new invention, the telescope, would prove the church wrong—as it did. He wanted to save them from embarrassment, but they wouldn't listen.

Q: *Can you believe in God* and *trust in science?*
A: It seems that today we have two choices: accept God through faith, choosing to believe what the Bible says (that God exists and loves us individually) or believe what science claims to prove (that there is no God).

But over the last 50 years, science has admitted that every discovery leads to more questions than answers. A century ago, many scientists believed they were on the verge of knowing all the answers regarding how we arrived on Earth. Now scientists say that the more they discover, the more they discover they don't know.

For example, if the force of gravity were slightly more, the universe would collapse on itself, like a balloon with the air sucked out of it. If the force of gravity were slightly less, it would have drifted apart as gases instead of forming solids. If the force that held protons and electrons together were the slightest bit weaker, hydrogen would not exist, and therefore water would not exist, and therefore life would not exist. At all levels, it seems that coincidence after coincidence after coincidence has made human life possible in a lonely, cold universe.

Many scientists now believe that the 15-billion-year construction of the universe has had one goal: producing human life. Science is proving that the odds of human life being produced by chance are like winning the same 10-million-dollar lottery every week for the next year. That's a big win!

It's true that belief in God truly takes a leap of faith, yet every year we see further proof that science—and reason—no longer stand in the way of a belief in God as the Creator of this universe.

JOURNAL TWO
THE HOW AND WHY
OF LIFE

Q: How did we come to be, and why do we exist?

A: As a human being, you're made up of one trillion cells.

How much is one trillion? To hold one trillion oranges, you'd need a box that's 250 miles long, 250 miles wide, and 250 miles high!

Even more amazingly, all these cells work together. Some cells grow hair; some grow teeth. Some cells don't begin to work until you become a teenager. Other cells wait until you're middle-aged. You have blood cells, heart muscle cells, liver cells, eye cells, brain neuron cells, and more.

Most amazing, all one trillion cells are the result of the one cell created when you were conceived. As Tyce's mom explained to him, the DNA in this first cell contains every bit of information needed for your body to grow.

Q: What exactly is DNA?

A: Deoxyribonucleic acid. It's life's building block.

DNA is shaped like a spiral staircase. In a human, the DNA ladder in one cell contains three billion "rungs." (If DNA rungs were the size of a real ladder's, those three billion rungs would circle the entire Earth—twice. Wow. Think about that!)

Because of its shape, DNA is able to replicate itself perfectly. When a cell needs to make a copy of itself, the DNA "ladder" unzips down the middle to form two halves. The result is two exact copies of the original. That's how one cell at conception can pass on the exact copy of its DNA to all trillion cells of a human.

Each different cell is able to specialize because it activates a different section of the DNA "ladder." These sections are called genes. Some genes trigger a cell to become hair cells. Other genes trigger a cell to become blood cells. And so on.

In one way, this method is extremely simple. After scientists discovered the double helix shape of DNA and everything else about it, they were able to run many experiments, including the ones mentioned by Tyce's mother.

In another way, DNA is incredible. The information stored in the DNA of just one cell would fill the hard drives of a million computers. The microscopic chemical reactions resulting from the DNA coding happen millions of times a day in your body.

DNA is so incredible that many scientists find it very difficult to believe that life was the result of accidental evolution. Like Tyce's mom, these scientists cannot help but look to God as our Creator.

Q: *So what does all this have to do with believing in God?*
A: Life itself is a humbling mystery. Think of it this way: We survive because of sunlight and water and dirt. Our bodies are nourished by carbohydrates from bread, which comes from wheat, which draws from sunlight and moisture and soil. Our bodies are strengthened by protein from the meat of animals, which feed upon plants. All of this is made possible by the water that falls from the skies and collects in rivers and lakes.

Sunlight, water, and dirt.

We forget how incredible it is because we see it and live it every day and give it little thought. We plunk down a few dollars for our hamburgers at a drive-through; we pick up milk from the grocery store; the sun throws off heat from 93 million miles away; the earth remains in its fixed distance from the sun—not too close, not too far, held by gravity that we can predict but not explain.

If you think of life this way, it's not hard to believe that such a world with such mystery exists because of the unseen hand of a Creator.

All of this leads to a much bigger question: why?

Although learning *how* we're on this earth is fascinating, learning *why* we're really here is the most wonderful purpose given to us as humans. Hope you enjoy the journey!

ABOUT THE AUTHOR

Sigmund Brouwer and his wife, recording artist Cindy
Morgan, and their daughters split living between Red Deer,
Alberta, Canada, and Nashville, Tennessee. He has written
several series of juvenile fiction and eight novels. Sigmund
loves sports and plays golf and hockey. He also enjoys visiting
schools to talk about books. He welcomes visitors to his Web
site at www.coolreading.com.